BARKING UP THE WRONG TREE

CAT AND MOUSE WHODUNITS
BOOK 3

EMILY JAMES

STRONGHOLD BOOKS

Emily James

authoremilyjames@gmail.com

www.authoremilyjames.com

This is a work of fiction. I made it up. You are not in my book. I probably don't even know you. If you're confused about the difference between real life and fiction, you might want to call a counselor rather than a lawyer because names, characters, places, and incidents in this book are a product of my twisted imagination. Real locales and public names are sometimes used for atmospheric purposes. Any resemblance to actual people, living or dead, or to businesses, companies, events, and institutions is completely coincidental.

Cover Design: Mariah Sinclair https://www.mariahsinclair.com

Published July 2023 by Stronghold Books

Ebook ISBN: 978-1-988480-61-9; Print Book ISBN: 978-1-988480-62-6

ALSO BY EMILY JAMES

Maple Syrup Mysteries

Sapped: A Maple Syrup Mysteries Prequel

A Sticky Inheritance

Bushwhacked

Almost Sleighed

Murder on Tap

Deadly Arms

Capital Obsession

Tapped Out

Bucket List

End of the Line

Slay Bells Ringing

(also contains a Cupcake Truck Mystery novella)

Rooted in Murder

Guilty or Knot

Stumped

Cupcake Truck Mysteries

Sugar and Vice

Dead Velvet Cake

Gum Drop Dead

1

I pushed open the convention center door, and a gust of wind slammed it back in my face. I readjusted the box of leashes, donation forms, and other leftovers from the shelter's annual Christmas fundraising event. Carrying out the rest of the stuff that belonged to the shelter was going to be great fun if it was half as wild outside as it seemed.

Using my whole body as leverage this time, I forced the door open. Snow nipped at my skin like the storm had tiny, razor-sharp teeth. The cold grabbed all the air from my lungs, and a hard shiver nearly shook the box from my grip. It just figured that the worse blizzard Michigan had seen in twenty years would blow in the same day we had to be an hour outside Arbor for this event.

I turtled my head down into my jacket collar and squinted into the swirling white. The convention center's lights and the parking lot's street lamps glowed off of a seemingly solid wall of snow. Forget hauling everything out here safely. I might not even be able to find my car. I hit the lock button on my key fob. My car horn honked, and I plowed through the snow in its general direction.

Only a handful of vehicles remained. Anyone who hadn't needed to stay to the end had left over an hour ago when the snow started piling up. Why hadn't I listened to Judith when she suggested ending the event early instead of telling her and Bob to head home and leave me and Tiffany to pack up?

Three cars lined up together appeared out of the squall, as if they were huddling together for warmth. Mine nestled in between Ryan's unmarked police cruiser and Tiffany's old beater. She'd come back inside from packing a load of stuff into her car less than five minutes ago, but the wind had already destroyed her tracks.

A drift nearly as high as my knees mounded up behind my car. Definitely a good thing I always kept a shovel, a window scraper, and non-clumping cat litter in my car in the winter. No way was I getting out of this winter wonderland otherwise.

I unlocked the trunk, but the snow piled on top made it too heavy to open. If the roads were anything like this, it was going to be a long, slow drive home. I balanced my box on one hip, brushed the trunk clean, and finally dropped my package inside. I pulled out all my winter emergency gear and put it in my front seat, just in case, then grabbed Orion's winter dog jacket and headed back for the convention center. Honestly, the people who were always wishing for a white Christmas clearly weren't the ones who had to shovel all the whiteness away.

Judith would call me the Grinch if she ever heard me say that. But that didn't make it less true. Snow was much more fun as a kid, when all you had to do was build forts and make snow angels.

My path back had partially drifted in. I stumbled into the convention center, my teeth chattering and out of breath. I brushed the snow off myself and stomped my boots mostly clean of snow. Maybe I should text Judith and ask her to have hot chocolate waiting for me when I got home. Assuming she wasn't at the shelter. Which she probably would be. She wouldn't have left Tiffany and me to do the clean-up ourselves if she hadn't been so worried that the shelter's backup generator wouldn't kick in if there were a power outage because of the storm. Apparently, they'd been having trouble with it.

"Dr. Stephenson?" a man's voice said tentatively from down the hall.

I straightened and turned. The convention center's janitor waited fifteen feet away, his hands clasped in front of him, as if he were afraid of coming any closer.

I surreptitiously wiped my sleeve across my face in case my nose was running, but all seemed good. The snow I'd gathered outside was melting off of me and dripping to the floor, though. "Sorry about the puddle."

"It's not that. Do you..." He swallowed hard, opened his mouth, swallowed again. Almost as if he were struggling not to throw up.

Was he ill? I frowned and closed the distance. "Is everything alright?"

He shook his head. A muscle popped in his cheek, suggesting he'd clenched his jaw. "Do you know where the policeman is?"

He had to mean Ryan. The convention center had donated the space for today, which was why we'd held the event an hour from Arbor, but they hadn't gone so far as to provide security. Ryan had volunteered, along with a couple other off-duty officers from Arbor. Ryan had told the other two to head home when the oncoming storm scared most of the crowd away.

The event closed to the public half an hour ago, so there couldn't be more than a handful of people remaining. Whatever he needed Ryan for, it probably wasn't to break up a brawl. With the bad weather, he was likely just wondering when we'd be done and he'd be able to lock up and go home. "I'm not sure, but we shouldn't be here much longer."

He shook his head again, and his gaze darted back down the hallway. "I really need to find him."

I leaned slightly to the side. The hallway was empty. I took a step in that direction.

The janitor shot his arm out, blocking my path. "Please, no."

Please, no? That was borderline weird. Part of me wanted to dodge around him and see what he was so determined to keep me away from. But that wouldn't reflect well on the shelter, and their Christmas fundraiser brought in a lot more when they didn't have to pay for a location to hold it. The convention center's size meant we'd been able to bring in vendors, hold a dog show, offer a microchip clinic, and host a lot of other special activities that drew a crowd—before the weather turned, anyway. Judith would be disappointed if I did something that meant the convention center wouldn't offer her the space again next year.

I motioned toward the main hall where we'd been set up and headed in that direction. "I'll help you look."

A woman screamed, the sound carrying down the hallway behind us, ricocheting off the high metal ceilings. My heart slammed into the bottom of my throat, and I spun around. Her screams kept coming.

The janitor swore behind me, loudly and not in a surprised way, like how other people might gasp. His curse word sounded more resigned and frustrated, as if the woman screaming was something he'd been trying to avoid. Whatever was going on, he already knew.

Why hadn't I followed my instinct to check things out when he'd been acting so weird? Asking directly for "the policeman" should have been a dead giveaway.

I sprinted back in the direction he'd come from when he first found me and asked for Ryan. The sound of someone else running came from behind me, heavy footsteps and gaining on me, likely a man's. Probably the janitor. A second set of footsteps joined in behind me.

The woman was still screaming.

Her cries cut off. Good or bad?

I picked up speed and skidded around the corner. My feet slipped, and my stomach plunged down. I instinctively put out my arms to break my fall.

Strong hands caught me before I could wipe out. I glanced up. Ryan stood next to me, but he wasn't looking at me.

I followed his gaze. A woman—presumably the screamer—stood at the bottom of a wide staircase that led up to the second level of the convention center. Her face was turned into the chest of the man who bred champion golden labs and had volunteered to judge the dog show. Mason was his name, I was pretty sure. I'd vaccinated his most recent litter of puppies a couple of months ago.

He had one arm around her, and he absently patted her back. His glasses were askew as if he'd also run here.

He stared at something on the floor.

My throat seemed to shrivel up and close. Not something. A person. A woman.

The janitor came to a stop beside us, gulping in air. Another woman and William Graudin, who owned the Arbor pet store, filtered in. Someone gasped. Someone else started to cry. I couldn't focus enough to figure out who.

"Is she dead?" The curvy woman with short blonde hair who now stood next to Mason asked. "Has anyone checked?"

Ryan softly let out a breath of air. He leaned closer to me. "Do you have a stethoscope in your bag?"

I nodded. "I'm the vet on site. I have everything I might need for an emergency."

He stared at me. My brain ground into motion again. Right. He wanted me to get it.

A few months ago, I'd gotten a bit of a reputation with Ryan for going into shock after I'd dealt with an emergency. He didn't seem to believe me that it'd only happened because I was close to the people involved. Now, unfortunately, I'd have my chance to prove him wrong.

I jogged back to the main hall. Tiffany hovered in the doorway, Orion's leash clutched in her hand. She looked like she'd been debating whether to stay put or follow the commotion, and only having to care for Orion had held her back.

She didn't need to see it if the person at the foot of the stairs was dead. Was she even in her twenties? Something like that could traumatize her for years.

"Stay here, okay?" I dodged past her and grabbed my bag. "I'll be back as soon as I can."

She nodded and obediently dropped into a chair.

By the time I got back to the stairs, Ryan had moved everyone away from the woman on the floor and knelt beside her. He'd gone into his police detective persona, and his posture and expression gave nothing away. The fact that he wasn't speaking to her did.

He was already on his phone, calling the situation in to the local police. This wasn't even his jurisdiction. He met my gaze and gave a tiny nod toward the woman on the floor.

I clenched my jaw. I could do this. He needed me to do this. I was the only medical professional here, after all. Granted, not a medical professional for people, but hearts beat the same in a dog as they did in a person.

I drew my stethoscope from my bag, breathed in for a count of four, and joined Ryan beside the woman. Her eyes were closed peacefully, but the angle of her neck was all wrong. Strands of her dyed red hair stuck to the shiny gloss on her lips.

She was the one who'd set up a food cart offering all-natural homemade dog meals. There'd been a line for her free samples all day. Victoria? I was pretty sure her name had been Victoria. She'd had a dog with her, hadn't she?

A tremor ran through my hands. *Do it. Just do it already, and then you can move away.*

I reached out my hand. Ryan stopped me, his hands swathed in gloves.

Of course. This was a potential crime scene, even though her location made it pretty clear she'd fallen down the stairs. One of her shoes had come off during the fall and lay nearby, the three-inch heel snapped from the base of the shoe. Those would be treacherous to walk in on flat ground, let alone down stairs.

I pulled a pair of gloves out of my bag and tugged them on. I gently slid my stethoscope down the neck of her silky caramel-colored blouse, over where my own doctor always put his stethoscope during a physical. Silence met my ears. No heartbeat. No breathing. I moved my stethoscope to the other side, just to make sure I wasn't letting the stress of the situation cause me to make a foolish mistake.

Nothing.

I'd done enough euthanasias to know what death sounded like. My eyes burned. What an awful way to die. She must have been so afraid in the moments of her fall. And for her family to lose her right before Christmas. No matter how many years passed, this time of year would never be the same for them.

Ryan watched me.

I cleared my throat. "She's gone."

The woman who'd been crying before broke into tears again. Maybe they'd been friends. She turned her head back into Mason's chest, so that only her long, straight dark hair remained visible. Mason was stiff in her clutches, as if he wanted to be somewhere else but was too much of a gentleman to push her away. The curvy woman next to them stared off into the distance, her gaze directed determinedly away from Victoria's body.

Ryan shifted his cell phone slightly. "No rush on the ambulance." He paused and tilted his head slightly to one side. "Could you repeat that please?"

A tension had entered his voice that hadn't been there before.

I leaned infinitesimally closer and strained my ears to hear the other end of the conversation.

"Roads...blizzard...secure..."

Ryan looked back over his shoulder, then to me. "I've got at least seven people here with me."

The words on the other end were too soft for me to hear anything other than "I'm sorry, Detective."

Ryan disconnected the call and slid his phone into his suit jacket pocket. He lifted a hand as if he intended to run it through his hair, only to realize that the gel holding his curls in place wouldn't allow it.

I swiped an alcohol pad over the diaphragm of my stethoscope and rolled my gloves off, turning them inside out. "What's going on?" I whispered.

"The roads are closed. There's so much snow they're impassible."

My brain quickly filled in the gaps. "No one can make it here? No paramedics? No other officers?"

Ryan nodded.

But that also meant... "We're all stuck here." I dropped my voice even further. "With a dead body?"

2
_____

The curvy woman pointed her finger at Ryan. "You can't detain us. It's against the law. We haven't done anything wrong."

Ryan's face stayed so calm he could have been made out of marble. "I'm not detaining you, ma'am. The roads aren't safe for travel."

She puffed her ample chest out. "Don't you *ma'am* me and think that'll make it alright."

I indulged in a daydream about making this woman sit in a corner like a naughty child and pursed my lips. Verbally putting her in her place wouldn't help Ryan's authority any. But really—she'd been insisting he had to let them leave for over five minutes now, and no amount of Ryan explaining that he wasn't the one preventing them from leaving seemed to make a difference. She was right, and he was wrong.

The woman who'd been crying scrubbed at the

mascara streaks under her eyes. "We're all going to die."
She hiccupped and hugged the oversized purse containing
her Chihuahua to her chest. "We're going to starve to
death. Our dogs are going to starve to death."

Her dog could survive on less than what Orion needed
for half a meal. If anyone should be concerned, it would be
me. Orion was by far the largest dog here, and he ate over
four cups of food a day. But we didn't need to worry about
that at least. "No one's going to starve. There's plenty of
food for us in the vending machines." I forced myself not
to look at Victoria's body. "And Victoria probably has
enough of her dog meals left to feed the dogs."

"That sounds like stealing." Graudin crossed his arms
over his chest. He turned to Ryan. "Are you going to let her
steal and justify it?"

I barely managed to keep from rolling my eyes. That
wasn't a surprising response coming from the man who
had security cameras all over his pet store and made
everyone who came in with anything larger than a clutch
leave it with the cashier while they shopped.

Crying Woman snuffled and pushed damp hair back
off her face. "I'd offer my homemade dog treats, but
someone ruined my entire inventory before the event even
started. I don't have any food for Lucy if we don't take the
dog meals."

The curvy woman huffed. "We're trapped here.
Surviving is what's important." She turned her pointer
finger on Graudin. "Besides, it's not like she's going to care.
She's dead."

Mason pushed his glasses up higher on his face. "That's cold."

"Even if we don't starve to death," Crying Woman's voice rose to a wail, "we'll freeze to death."

"That's not the kind of cold he meant," the curvy woman said.

"I know that. I'm not stupid!"

It probably wouldn't be appropriate to turn a hose on them to break them up the way I would a dog fight. But it sure would be satisfying.

"Detective?" a soft male voice said.

Ryan and I turned in tandem as if we'd practiced it, even though I definitely wasn't the detective here.

The janitor held his hand tentatively in the air as if he were back in school. "The building automatically turns down to fifty-five at night. I can't change it. But I do have keys to the cafeteria. Would you like me to see if there's anything in the fridges?"

"More theft. That food wasn't purchased for this event." Graudin stalked toward one of the exterior doors. "The rest of you can do what you want, but I'm leaving."

"Wait!" Crying Woman scurried after him. "Take me with you!"

Did it make me a horrible person that the first thing that crossed my mind wasn't their safety but that it'd be more peaceful for the rest of us if those two did leave? Maybe they could take the curvy woman with them. With only Ryan, Mason, the janitor, Tiffany, and me here, we'd have a more peaceful time of things.

Tiffany. I glanced around. She stood quietly at the edge of the group, far enough away to keep Orion calm despite all the arguing. When I hadn't returned, she must have come looking for me. But when had she gotten here? She hadn't made a peep even though there was a dead body on the floor.

Ryan followed Graudin and Crying Woman. "It's an offence punishable by law to drive on a closed road."

"Ticket me, then," Graudin shouted back over his shoulder. "It's better than staying here and becoming a thief."

Graudin stormed out the door, followed by Crying Woman, Ryan, and then everyone else, jostling for position to see if he managed it. I met Tiffany's gaze, shrugged, and trailed along.

She pointed at Orion. "We'll stay here, where it's warm."

So she wasn't afraid of being left alone with a dead body, either. The girl had nerves of concrete. I'd underestimated her.

I caught up to Ryan at the front of the pack. "Aren't you going to stop him?"

"Short of pulling my gun on him, I don't think I can." He raised his eyebrows. "And that seems like overkill, don't you think?"

I would have stuck my tongue out at him if it wasn't so cold that I was afraid it might have frozen in that position. Good thing I still had my winter coat on.

Graudin climbed into a truck not far from the

entrance. The thing had massive snow tires covered in chains. Crying Woman and her chihuahua clambered in the other side, having to use the running boards and a handle to pull herself in.

The wind shifted and burned my face and hands. I edged closer to Ryan's bigger body. "This is a good test. If anything can make it out of here, that monster should."

He glanced down at me. "Are you trying to use me as a wind block?"

I shrugged. "Isn't that what friends are for?"

He sighed in that way he had that made it sound like a laugh. "Hopefully this doesn't take long or we'll have frostbite to deal with. But some people have to learn the hard way."

Graudin fired up his truck. Apparently, he had enough faith in his beast of a machine that he didn't feel the need to shovel around it. The engine revved, and his tires spun. The truck lurched forward a foot, then stopped. His tires dug into the ground, kicking up snow.

Our little crowd moved back, despite being far enough away that the snow didn't come close to hitting anyone.

Graudin's truck rocked back and forth. He must have been shifting it between forward and reverse. If his truck was having this much trouble, my car most definitely wasn't getting out of here tonight. I could practically drive underneath him.

His tires caught, and the truck jumped forward again, hit another snow bank, and refused to move, no matter how much he gunned the engine.

The engine shut off. The doors didn't open immediately. Crying Woman was probably trying to convince him to try again.

Graudin's door opened first. He dropped to the ground. Crying Woman gingerly climbed out as well. They trudged back over to where the rest of us stood.

"You're all idiots for standing out here in the cold," Graudin said.

Maybe, but it kind of felt like it was worth it to see him fail after he refused to listen to Ryan.

Ryan motioned everyone back toward the building. "I have to count the vehicles in the lot to make sure we've accounted for everyone. While I'm gone, Dr. Stephenson is in charge of getting us all safely settled in for however long we need to be here."

I was in charge? We sure had come a long way from when we first met and he suspected me of murdering my ex-fiancé.

Crying Woman hunched over her bag, clearly protecting her tiny dog from the worst of the weather. "But what are we going to do about Victoria?"

———

I RAN down the list I'd made on my phone. Everyone had already brought in any blankets or clothing they had in their cars. I'd asked Leo the janitor to check out what was in the cafeteria, the way he'd suggested. Mason was counting the bottles of water left in the coolers that had been donated for the event so we could ration them fairly. Tiffany was working with the curvy woman—whose name turned out to be Darcy—to go through Victoria's supplies and figure out how we needed to divide up the food between Orion, the chihuahua who belonged to Simone, and Victoria's missing dog. Assuming I could manage to locate him. I'd asked everyone, and no one had seen him since before Leo found Victoria's body. No one seemed to know his name, either. Best guess was he got scared when she fell and ran off to hide somewhere.

The building was a sizeable one. It'd take me a long time to search it alone, but the only people left without tasks were Graudin and Simone.

Graudin sat in a corner, arms crossed, glaring at everyone who moved. Simone lay on her back on a pile of the collected clothes and blankets, practicing some deep breathing so she didn't hyperventilate. She'd put her chihuahua in a tiny purple coat with a hood, and the dog had curled up into a ball on Simone's stomach.

Should I try to enlist them to help me? Graudin caught me looking at him, and he scowled.

On second thought, I'd rather go alone. I could use the time to call Judith and let her know what was going on, anyway.

I left the convention hall.

"Come," I called as I walked down the hallway, dialing Judith's number. "Come, doggie."

A lot of the doors along here went into storage closets and bathrooms. A dog wouldn't have been able to open them. I'd lap the first floor anyway and then check upstairs. Victoria had obviously been up there, since she fell down the stairs, even though the event had been confined to the first floor.

Judith's phone went straight to voicemail. I left a message. I couldn't call Bob's cell. He'd been lamenting earlier today because he'd accidentally left it in his car when he and Judith decided to take her car instead. I called the shelter and got the answering machine there. Was she still stuck on the roads? The image of Graudin's truck spinning its tires filled my head. But surely Judith had made it home safely. It hadn't been snowing heavily when she and Bob left.

I called Keith. Having a boyfriend who lived next door could be really convenient, and not only because he'd taken to cutting our lawn during the warmer months. He, thankfully, answered on the second ring.

"Can you look out into our driveway and see if Judith's car is there?"

After dating for almost eight months, at least he didn't hassle me anymore for occasionally skipping the *hellos*. Sometimes, even though it was the polite way to start a conversation, it didn't seem important enough to spend time on.

A soft swish as if he were pulling back the curtains. "Your driveway's empty."

My lungs deflated, and I couldn't get air back in. What if they were stuck in a snowdrift somewhere? They could run out of gas and freeze to death before any help came if the roads were closed. Or their tailpipe could get clogged with snow without them knowing it, and they could die from carbon monoxide poisoning. Judith knew not to run her car without checking for obstructions, didn't she? I should have told her that when I put together her winter driving emergency kit.

I shouldn't have been so hard on Simone. Anyone's mind could run in anxiety-ridden circles if they weren't careful.

I breathed in slowly for a count of four, held it for a count of four, and breathed out, emptying my lungs completely, until breathing seemed natural again.

Judith and Bob were out of my control right now. Panicking wouldn't help them. Besides, with the storm picking up, she and Bob probably went straight to the shelter. They could easily be too busy with making sure the backup generator was working to answer the phone at a time when the shelter was supposed to be closed.

"Is the power out?" I asked Keith.

"All over town." A slight pause. "When do you think you'll be home? I was hoping we could talk more tonight. I could order us a pizza. A couple places are still open."

Talk more tonight. Not-so-subtle code for *continue the conversation that you've been avoiding.* I held back a snort. Finally, the storm was good for something. I needed more time. "I'm stuck here at least for tonight. They closed the roads because of the storm."

A wordy silence filled Keith's end. Almost like he

thought I was making it up. Or like I could have done something to avoid being trapped here.

Tension pooled around my temples. "You can check the MDOT website if you don't believe me." My tone came out more confrontational than I'd expected.

"It's not that I don't believe you." He paused again. "We are going to continue to talk about this, aren't we?"

Not an unreasonable request. An adult request, to be honest. I couldn't dodge around it forever. I shouldn't. But I wanted my thoughts to feel less jumbled before we did. "Yes. Absolutely."

"Stay safe." The tightness had left his voice. "I love you."

"Stay warm. We'll talk when I get home. I promise."

I disconnected the call. I should have said *I love you* back. Keith had to have noticed. It was just that every time I tried, the words lodged in my throat like a spring ice flow backing up a river. As if I needed more proof that I was defective when it came to relationships, that should have been all the evidence necessary. Maybe I couldn't even love new people. Maybe the way Tonya raised me and the way Sebastian cheated on me had broken that part of me.

I shoved my phone in my pocket. For now, I had an excuse not to think about it for a little longer at least. I had a dog to find.

Which would be a lot easier if I knew his name. "Come, Buddy. Charlie. Max." If I ran through the names I heard most often at the vet clinic, I'd at least have a chance of hitting on it. "Here, Duke. Bear." Hmm, probably not one of those. Her dog had looked like a Yorkshire Terrier. "Teddy?"

No whimper in response. No clatter of nails clicking on the floor. The only noise was the whir of air through the pipes as the furnace kept things warm and the wind beating against the exterior walls as the storm tried to break its way inside. I reached a staircase on the far side of the building from where Victoria fell and climbed them.

What had she been doing up here, anyway? This floor was all offices and off-limits to people using the convention center. And it would have been empty today since it was a Saturday. Had her dog gotten loose and she was chasing after him? If she'd been trying to run up the stairs in her heels, that could explain how she'd fallen.

A scraping *clink* like something sharp grating on metal carried faintly down the hallway.

I followed the sound. The overhead lights for the second level were off. Only the regularly spaced emergency lights along the ceiling gave off a faint glow.

Barking so shrill it left an echo in my ears drowned out everything else. I stopped and squinted down the dim hallway.

Ten feet away, a Yorkie huddled close to the wall. His tan coat had been trimmed short and spiky, rather than left long and flowing, just like the dog I'd seen with Victoria.

I moved closer and knelt down. "Hey, little guy. Would you like to come with me?"

His barking kicked up even louder. Not an unusual

reaction for a Yorkie if they hadn't been trained from puppyhood about when it was appropriate to bark and when it wasn't. Though, to be fair, he'd witnessed his owner's death. Almost any dog would be stressed and afraid in this situation.

He should still have his leash on him. Maybe if I could get hold of it, he might feel more secure.

I edged around him, leaving enough space so that he didn't feel more threatened than he already did. He backed away from me, closer to the old radiator next to him.

I squinted. Was his leash tangled in the radiator? That would explain why he hadn't shown up downstairs before this.

"I'm going to have to get closer to let you free, okay?"

His little body bounced as he continued to bark at me. He backed up as far as his leash would allow. The leash drew taunt.

Given that there were more modern vents in the ceiling, the radiator probably wasn't functional anymore. I wrapped my hand in my sleeve anyway and tapped the metal. Cool to the touch.

I unwrapped my hand and knelt. He'd somehow managed to get his leash snarled in a way that he'd never have been able to free himself from, short of chewing through his leash. Based on the fraying near the radiator, he'd tried that already. The leash was nylon, which I hated because a medium to large dog could slice your palm right open with them if they pulled suddenly. But I had to give nylon leashes credit for being sturdy.

The leash had snarled behind the radiator, with the loop at the end wedged tightly between the radiator and the wall. The rest of it threaded through pipes at the top. I wriggled the loop out and unwound the leash, him barking at me the entire time. It was a miracle my ears weren't bleeding. Next time someone asked me why I preferred big dogs, I was going to point to this. Big dogs might have louder barks, but they weren't nearly as shrill.

His leash popped free, and I sighed. Finally.

"Alright, until I know your real name, I'm going to call you Teddy." I stood. "Do you know how to *heel*, Teddy?"

Teddy trotted along beside me. Barking.

How was that even possible? He was going to lose his voice if he kept this up.

Since Ryan had blocked the staircase Victoria fell down with some rope he'd scrounged, I led Teddy back the way I'd come. We took the opposite stairway and followed the hallway around until we reached Victoria's staircase.

Victoria's body still lay at the bottom of the stairs, but Ryan had covered her with a sheet. Ryan stood on the other side of the staircase, his phone to his ear. I backed up. He wouldn't be able to hear anything the person on the other end was saying if I got too much closer. There was no way Victoria had properly socialized Teddy as a puppy. No dog should bark for this long for no reason.

I tied Teddy to the doorknob of a locked door and moved away. At somewhere around ten to fifteen feet, he stopped barking and dropped into a sit position, panting.

"Is that Victoria's dog?" Ryan approached from behind me.

I stuck out my arm to stop his progress. "Don't get any closer. I still have phantom barking in my ears. How are you not deaf from firing your gun in the past? That has to be louder than one small dog."

Ryan took a precautionary step back. "I wear hearing protection at the firing range."

My earmuffs were in my car. What I wouldn't give for them now. But all that snow... were they really worth going out in the snow again?

I glanced down the hallway in the direction of the door that led to the parking lot and caught a glimpse of the sheet covering Victoria again. "I assumed when you said you were going to take care of her that you meant you were going to move her body somewhere less public."

Ryan tucked his phone back into his jacket pocket. "Not yet. I did finally get permission to pick the lock on the security office door. I'm hoping the security footage caught Victoria's fall."

Security footage meant cameras. I looked up at the ceiling and turned in a circle. "I didn't notice any cameras."

Ryan caught me by the shoulders, stopping my motion. "You're going to make yourself dizzy doing that." He redirected me and pointed up at a small black box nestled near the ceiling. "See it now?"

It was more like a remote control on a tiny black stick. That was absolutely not what I expected a security camera to look like.

I could have saved him the trouble of getting permission to pick the locks to access the recordings if he'd asked me. "You don't need to pick the lock. Leo, the janitor, has a set of keys. He probably has one for the security office so that he can clean in there."

I took a step in the direction of the cafeteria.

Ryan's hand closed gently around my wrist and brought me to a stop before I could get any farther away. "I know Leo has keys. I didn't ask him because I don't want anyone to know I'm looking at the footage until we know for sure that Victoria's fall was an accident."

3

―――――――

"Of course her fall was an accident."

The words shot out of my mouth instinctively the same way I might have said *It wasn't me* as a kid if I were found standing over a broken plate.

But why *had* Victoria been going up to that floor? She could have been meeting someone. They'd have had privacy on the second floor because it wasn't being used. And presumably most people would use the handrail when climbing the stairs, which made falling accidentally unlikely. As precarious as her shoes were, she'd likely mastered walking in them, even on stairs. No one wore heels like that for a day-long event unless they were experienced. I couldn't wear heels for more than an hour without developing a limp.

A heavy weight settled in my chest and refused to move. "Wasn't it an accident?"

Ryan squeezed my arm gently as if he could see me

being sucked down into the worst possible scenario. The warmth of his hand dissolved some of the pressure on my lungs. "Most likely. But I have to treat her body and the scene differently depending on whether her death was accidental or suspicious. I've already photographed everything. I just can't move her if there's any chance someone did this to her. We could lose material evidence that would identify the killer."

I glanced again at where Victoria's body lay, then quickly away. Her body was only a shell. The soul that had made her Victoria was already gone. But it still seemed disrespectful somehow to leave her out in the open, like she'd been of no more value than trash someone abandoned by the side of the road.

If Ryan couldn't move her until we were sure this wasn't a murder, then we'd go check the security footage to get the proof he needed. "I'm coming with you."

"You do know you're not actually a member of the police force, right? You can't become an honorary member the way you can get an honorary degree." His delivery was so deadpan that I couldn't tell if he were teasing me or serious.

I stepped back into range of Teddy, and his barking kicked up. I pointed a finger at my ear. "What's that? I can't hear you."

I saw more than heard Ryan sigh. His mouth moved in what looked like him saying *Why do I bother?* He motioned me to follow him down the hallway, back toward the other staircase.

I let Teddy's leash out as far as it would go. He kept barking anyway. I fell into step with Ryan. It was a good thing we didn't need to be stealthy about this. "You don't happen to have any ear plugs?" I yelled. "Like the kind you'd use at the firing range?"

He shook his head. "If I did, trust me, I'd be putting them in my own ears right now."

When we reached the security office door, Ryan pulled a lock-picking kit from his jacket pocket. "You're going to have to tie her dog up somewhere. If the recordings have sound, we need to hear it."

Teddy would probably be glad for a break from his constant protests anyway. I secured him one door down and stepped away. The quiet felt better than sinking into a hot bath after a long day.

Ryan slid his tools into the lock and wriggled them around. He adjusted and tried again. The lock gave way with a *snick*. Even watching carefully, I couldn't figure out what he'd done.

I held my hand out toward his tool kit, palm up. "Can you teach me how to do that?"

He leveled a stare at me. "There's no situation in which you need to pick a lock."

I could think of several situations in which I might want to pick a lock, and most of them were legal. "What if I get locked out of my house?"

"You're telling me neither Judith nor Ellery have another key?" He had me there. Ellery kept a key to our house hanging with her own keys since it seemed safer to leave a spare with a neighbor rather than hidden some-where outside.

"What if I'm worried about Mr. Clunes and I want to check to make sure he's okay?"

"Call his building superintendent. Going into some-one's home without permission is breaking and entering."

"What if—"

Ryan held up his hand, but his lips twitched at the corners as if it were taking everything he had not to smile. "Get inside before I change my mind about letting you watch this video with me."

For a second, my feet refused to move. The video we were about to watch would show Victoria dying, whether she'd fallen or was pushed. My desire to know for sure what had happened had clearly blocked out the thought of what I'd offered to watch—insisted I be allowed to watch. Did I really need to see that? I'd never be able to forget it. Ever.

Ryan had the door open, holding it for me. He let it slide partway shut. "You don't have to." His voice was soft, all teasing gone. "You don't have anything to prove here."

I brought my gaze up to his. His look was as soft as his voice. How was this the same man who'd suspected me of murder earlier this year? Who I'd once thought was the biggest jerk I'd ever met? Had he said *you don't have to* a few months ago, I would have heard it as a challenge. His tone of voice wouldn't have mattered. I'd have leaped into it to prove to him that I was better than he assumed I was. Regardless of the consequences.

But I knew him well enough now to know this wasn't him saying I wasn't strong enough. This wasn't him saying I was a coward. This was him saying that no one should have to see what we were about to. He had no choice. Death was an unfortunate part of his job, the same way it was for a doctor or a paramedic. I could walk away, and he wouldn't think less of me for it.

I would still think less of myself, though. Just not for the reason he might assume. He'd been there for me more than once when things went sideways. When I'd been covered in blood. When I'd been attacked and shot at. When no one else believed me.

The least I could do was stand next to him now. He was here without the usual team he'd have when dealing with a death, and he'd have no opportunity at the end of the day for privacy or however he dealt with the evil he bumped up against every day in his job. At the end of today, he'd still have to take care of everyone trapped here with us.

I shook my head. "I'm coming. You shouldn't have to watch it alone."

An expression I couldn't read flickered across his face. He opened the door again, and I went in first.

A wall of monitors made the room glow as if we'd stepped into an old black and white movie. The cameras showed multiple angles of the convention hall, where almost everyone now congregated. That made sense, with the convention hall being the most used part of the convention center.

The other monitors didn't even begin to cover the rest of the building. None of them seemed to cover the second floor at all.

"Did whoever you spoke to say the stairs are even *on* the security footage?"

Ryan pointed to two small monitors down by his left side. I leaned closer. Both showed part of empty stairwells. The stairs I'd gone up when I'd been looking for Teddy were only half in the frame, as if the camera wasn't properly installed. Anyone walking up the right side, the way a right-handed person normally would, wouldn't have been caught on camera. Good thing that wasn't the camera recording the stairs Victoria fell down. As it was, the bottom of the stairs she fell down weren't on the screen. Perhaps that was a blessing since we wouldn't need to see the moment Victoria's life ended.

"They have the cameras mostly to prevent stealing and discourage fights or vandalism on the main level." Ryan flipped open his notebook and pressed buttons, presumably following whatever instructions he'd been given for operating the system. "Those angles are the best we're going to get."

A large screen beside me flickered to life. I swiveled my chair around to face it.

Ryan rolled another chair over and sat next to me. "The video feed is on a forty-eight-hour loop. I've changed the settings now so that it won't record anything more. Can't risk accidentally recording over the footage."

Ryan tapped something into the keyboard, and an

image of a stairwell filled the screen in front of us. The bottom of the image had a date and timestamp. The timestamp moved forward, the image flickering slightly at the edges even though nothing else changed.

Occasionally a person went up or down, their legs and arms moving unrealistically fast as Ryan zipped through Friday. The stairs grew quiet and dark as night passed. Fewer people went up and down on Saturday, even though Judith said this year was the fundraiser's best yet. Leo passed a few times, once coming back with a mop and bucket. That had to be the first time one of the dogs peed on the floor. A mother with two small children went by later, probably accidentally thinking the bathrooms were up there.

I watched the timestamp and held up my hand. "Slow it down. This is around the last time I saw Victoria in the convention hall."

Ryan pressed a button, and the recording slowed to normal speed. He laid his notebook on the desk. "What was she doing when you last saw her?"

I rolled through my memories of the evening. Judith and Bob had already left by that point, as had almost everyone else. "Packing up, I think."

"Did you see anyone talk to her? Did she leave with anyone?"

Tiffany and I were packing up the items that belonged to the shelter, and I was trying to make sure Orion didn't wander off. He'd been intent on snuffling up bits of any food people had dropped. "I'm sorry. I don't remember. I wasn't paying much attention to her."

At the time, there hadn't been a reason to. She was one vendor among many. I'd had no reason to think someone would kill her. And, really, I'd been more focused on the snow and what the drive home would be like.

Victoria came into frame on the screen, walking up the stairs. Teddy calmly trotted along beside her.

I checked the timestamp again. This would have been happening around the time I was going out to my car and realizing how hard it was snowing.

Victoria reached the top of the stairs and stopped on the landing. She draped Teddy's leash over her arm, instead of continuing to hold onto it. Teddy moved out of frame slightly, then came back and lay down beside Victoria's feet. His head shifted down as if he were chewing at an itch on one of his paws. "Her dog doesn't look upset."

The whole scene looked so peaceful—like a poorly made horror film where the music didn't warn you in advance that something bad was about to happen.

Victoria's hands moved as if she were using them to punctuate something she was saying.

"No sound?" We could have brought Teddy in after all if there wasn't. Though the quiet did make it easier to concentrate.

Ryan paused the recording and pulled a binder off a shelf as if he'd been told exactly where to find it. He probably had. He flipped it open, turned a few pages, and read for a minute.

"The system doesn't have audio capabilities." He restarted the recording and leaned forward, closer to the screen. "But she's definitely talking to someone."

Whoever it was stood beyond the camera's range. The company that set the cameras up should refund their fee, given how shoddy the coverage was. "Maybe they didn't come forward because they were afraid of being accused of pushing her. They probably didn't know about the cameras."

"Maybe. We'll see."

Victoria's hands stilled, then moved again dismissively. The image was small and wasn't facing her head-on, but it seemed like she was smiling mockingly at whoever she was talking to. The lift of her cheeks and the tilt of her head suggested haughtiness.

She shook her head. The movement was slow, as if she couldn't believe the person would even ask her what they had. She said something.

Hands flashed into the image and shoved her. Victoria's arms shot out, grabbing for anything and connecting only with air. She was either too far from the railing to stop her fall or, in her panic, hadn't thought to reach to the side.

I sucked in a sharp breath and squeezed my eyes shut. Why would someone do that? The act clearly hadn't been premeditated, but they still must have intended to kill her. You didn't push someone backward down a tall flight of stairs if you didn't mean to hurt them. How angry must they have needed to be with her to do something like that?

"I paused the video," Ryan said. "You can look again."

I slowly opened one eye, then the other. He'd stopped the video the second after Victoria toppled backward. She hung suspended at an unnatural angle.

The arms of the person who shoved her were once again gone from the frame. He or she hadn't regretted the action enough in that split second to try to stop Victoria's fall.

"Could you tell..." My voice cracked. I cleared my throat and tried again. "Could you tell if it was a man or a woman?"

Ryan shook his head. "Maybe once the techs enhance it we might be able to see some distinguishing feature, but right now, it's too small and grainy. I'll take pictures and notes on what everyone's wearing for reference."

Even once the techs got it, there was only so much they could do. If the resolution wasn't high enough, they wouldn't be able to pull out details because those details wouldn't have been recorded in the first place. "Did the video of the other staircase catch them going down?"

Ryan tapped a command into the keyboard. The recording of the other stairwell replaced Victoria on the screen. Ryan zipped through the footage until an hour before Victoria's death. Five minutes before she fell, the camera caught a flash of a hand belonging to someone climbing the stairs. We watched it back three times but couldn't pick out if it belonged to a man or a woman. The person managed to stay out of the recording on their way down as well. Ryan moved the video forward until long after we were all together around Victoria's body. There was no sign of anyone coming back down.

I slumped back in my chair. "Great. So we know someone killed her, but we have no clue who."

"That's not entirely true." Ryan touched a finger to the bottom of the screen, next to the timestamp. "We know that whoever killed her is trapped in this building with us until the storm clears. I checked the parking lot. Every car is accounted for as belonging to one of us, and Mr. Graudin proved that no one could have left after shoving Victoria down the stairs. The snow was already too deep."

The temperature in the room seemed to drop by ten degrees, and I shivered. Too bad it was too early in the evening for me to blame it on the automated thermostat.

One of the six other people here with us was a murderer. "Not comforting."

Ryan turned off the screen with the paused recording. "We do have an advantage. The murderer doesn't realize that we know Victoria's death was a murder."

Which meant that whoever killed her didn't have their guard up the way they would after the police officially declared Victoria's death suspicious. "So we keep it that way until we can figure out who it was."

Ryan's lips parted slightly, as if he were about to say that there wasn't a *we*. That he was the police detective, and he would be the one trying to solve this crime. He looked at me long enough that heat built in my cheeks.

His shoulders came down slightly as if everything he thought about saying had evaporated. "Exactly."

4

I peeked out the security office door. Teddy lay calmly stretched out on the floor where I left him, licking himself. "Where do we start?"

"Alibis." Ryan turned off the screen. The image of the empty stairway vanished. "That will help narrow it down."

I closed the security office door. "That sounds like you weren't with anyone at the time."

Ryan loosened his tie slightly—something he wouldn't do around anyone else here. This might be his last moment to let his guard down until the weather cleared and the roads reopened. People felt safer if they didn't have to think about certain professionals being people with feelings and troubles of their own who got tired, who hurt, and who sometimes loved their jobs but sometimes also hated them. In this case, when we had no help from outside, they had to see Ryan as law enforcement rather than as a fellow human being. We had a better chance of everyone staying calm if they did.

Ryan rolled his neck from side to side and rotated his shoulders as if the weight of responsibility on them was tangible.

My fingers twitched. I could easily use my thumbs to take the knots out of his shoulders, but there was a niggling sense in the back of my mind that I shouldn't. I could still see the look on Keith's face when he found Ryan with his arm around me after I'd nearly been shot. It'd been entirely innocent comfort from a friend, but I'd promised Keith I'd be more careful about giving the wrong impression. As a pastor's girlfriend, he liked to remind me, I couldn't do whatever I wanted and only think about the repercussions later.

Ryan stopped rolling his shoulders and grimaced. "I was in the bathroom. I stepped in something outside that I'm pretty sure was dog poop. Someone thought they didn't need to clean up because the snow would hide it."

Or they thought their dog was so small that no one would notice. Since I didn't smell anything in the confines of the room, at least he'd gotten it off. "I was taking a load of stuff out to my car, so I can't vouch for anyone, either. Though it would have been hard for Tiffany to do it since she had Orion."

"She could have tied him up for a few minutes."

Sometimes I hated it when he made sense.

That meant we had five people unaccounted for. Six if we included Tiffany. And until we could prove otherwise, we had to approach it as if any one of them could be the killer.

My mouth and throat went dry as if I'd been talking for hours without any water. More than one person had done something suspicious. Graudin had tried to leave, despite the snow. Tiffany hadn't been shocked or upset by the sight of Victoria's body. Leo had acted strangely when I'd met up with him in the hall, and maybe he wanted to be the one to report finding Victoria so he wouldn't look guilty. Simone was so upset she was practically non-responsive now.

And that was assuming the guilty party would look suspicious. They might be extra careful *not* to do something that would draw attention, like Mason and Darcy.

Hopefully a couple of the others had been together. Otherwise, we had a lot of suspects to sort through.

Ryan tightened his tie back up and stood. "I'll ask about alibis under the guise of trying to figure out if Victoria might have been sick or inebriated and that's why she fell. I can tell them the tox screen will be too late to detect any substances in her system, and I'll need it for my report. Did they see or hear anything prior to her fall?"

That might still make the murderer suspicious, but I didn't have a better idea. "I can try to direct the conversations to see if anyone might have had motive. Subtly," I added before Ryan could tell me not to make myself a target. Subtlety wasn't known as my strong suit. "If I can get people talking about Victoria, I'll at least be able to pick up on how everyone felt about her."

Ryan opened the door and held it for me. "Will you scowl at me if I tell you to be careful?"

A smile edged across my lips. He was so predictable sometimes. "You don't need to. Like you said, whoever killed Victoria still thinks we assume it was an accident. It'd be pretty hard to hide hurting me as a second accident."

Ryan rolled his gaze to the ceiling as if praying for me. "You'd be surprised at what murderers think they can get away with."

———

BY THE TIME I got back to the convention hall, everyone was there except for Ryan and Leo, who must have still been hunting for food in the cafeteria.

Poor Ryan. The second we'd stepped within Teddy's radius after coming out of the security office, he'd barked incessantly again. Ryan had taken Teddy in the vague hope that if he allowed him to see Victoria's body, he might move from agitation to grief.

I passed Victoria's booth. Darcy and Tiffany had written out all the meals and assigned them to each of the three dogs based on size. We'd need to move the food from the large, wheeled cooler Victoria had it in to the fridge in the cafeteria, but the dogs had enough food to last through Monday if need be.

Simone still lay on the floor on her back, one arm draped over her eyes like she was some sort of fainting starlet from Hollywood's golden age. The others sat near her in a circle, playing cards in all their hands. Orion's tail thumped on the floor, and he got up from his spot behind Tiffany to come to me.

She let his leash go, her gaze intent on her hand of cards, a frown on her face. "What's the best hand again?"

Both Graudin and Mason sighed as if she'd asked that question enough times that they wanted to throw their cards at her.

"I told you we should have played Spades instead of poker," Darcy grumbled.

I scratched Orion behind the ears and scooped his leash up. "Detective MacIntosh sent me to ask if anyone knows who Victoria's next of kin might be. The police need to contact them."

The four in the circle all shook their heads.

"She had a boyfriend." Simone removed her arm from her eyes and raised her head slightly, looking in my direction. She lowered her head to the floor again but didn't cover her face back up. "I overheard her telling someone on her phone that she was hoping the snow wouldn't stop her from making it to his house tonight. His wife was going to be away with the kids, and they'd have the whole place to themselves if she could get there."

Darcy snorted. "I doubt a *married* boyfriend is going to be her next of kin."

Too bad the boyfriend or the wife weren't here, though. Adultery would have been a clear motive. Either the boyfriend could have killed her to keep her from telling his wife, or the wife could have killed her in a jealous rage after Victoria refused to stay away from her husband.

But based on Victoria's conversation, the wife was far from here with her children as alibis, and the boyfriend was waiting for her somewhere else. Of the men here, Leo and Graudin wore wedding rings. But if either of them was the boyfriend, she'd have been more likely to tell the person on the phone that she was hoping they'd be able to make it to a hotel after the event ended.

Still, I could pass that information on to Ryan. Someone at the police department could get Victoria's call log and find out which married men she'd been regularly calling.

"I'm out." Darcy laid her cards on the floor. She leaned back, propping herself up on her hands. "From the sound of it, we should be grateful we're not stuck here with Victoria. She was clearly an awful person. What kind of woman knowingly sleeps with someone else's husband?"

"Not everyone who cheats is an awful person." Tiffany moved her cards closer to her face, as if looking at the cards that way would help her figure out whether she had a good hand or not. She sounded like she was only half paying attention to what she was saying. "People make mistakes."

Mason rapped the edge of his cards on the floor. "Tell that to my sister. She did everything for her husband, only to have him cheat on her. Now she's living in my guest room because she's been out of her career field for nearly

5

A scrabbling sensation grew at the bottom of my throat, as if my heart was tired of being here and wanted to escape. Leo should be here. He'd offered to check the cafeteria for food. Once he finished, he was supposed to come right back to the main hall.

I drew Orion closer to me. Had something happened to Leo? Maybe we were stuck in a blizzard with a serial killer.

"I'm being ridiculous, aren't I?" Orion looked up at me and perked his ears. "Serial killers make up less than one percent of all murderers. We have a better chance of dying in a plane crash."

Orion tilted his head like he was trying to figure out if all those words meant it was almost time for food. Poor boy would need to wait a little longer.

I walked back out into the hallway. If something had happened to Leo, what did that mean? Everyone else was in the convention hall. Could another person be hiding in the building? Ryan had said he'd accounted for all the cars, so that didn't seem likely. Plus, I couldn't be sure that no one had left the convention hall in the time Ryan and I were away. Though if Leo had been attacked, then we should easily be able to figure out who'd left the convention hall. We'd have our killer, but at Leo's expense.

I sucked in a long breath and paid attention to the way my lungs stretched and my ribs moved. Judith would tell me I was taking things to extremes again. There could be a lot of reasons Leo wasn't where he was supposed to be. Maybe he'd gone to the bathroom. Or since he knew we were setting up for an overnight stay, perhaps he had other supplies he felt would be useful. He could be collecting those.

Those types of things seemed to be stored upstairs. I'd check there first before I let my imagination go any further.

I trotted down the hall and took the stairs on the opposite side from where Victoria lay. Teddy's barks weren't vibrating the entire building anymore, so he'd either settled down or Ryan had needed to tie him up at a distance again.

I reached the top of the stairs and slid to a stop. Leo stood at the door to the security office. He had a key in the lock. He tried to turn it, but the key didn't budge. He pulled the key out and inserted a different one.

There was only one reason I could think of that he'd be trying to get into that room now.

"Ryan!" I yelled as loud as I could.

Leo jerked away from the door and fumbled with the keys. He jammed them back onto his belt and buckled it. "I can explain."

He took a step toward me.

My heart hit the front of my chest. "Stop. Don't come any closer." I was standing at the top of a staircase, the same way Victoria had been before someone pushed her. All it would take would be for him to shove me, too, and I could end up like her. "Ryan!"

His name came out more as a scream than a yell this time.

"Zoe!" Ryan sprinted down the hallway from the other end.

He must have taken the stairs two at a time and jumped the ropes he'd put up. His gaze landed on me, then on Leo. He stopped ten feet from where Leo stood.

His hand moved toward his hip where his gun rested under his suit jacket. "What's going on?"

I pointed toward the door. "He was trying to get into the security office."

Leo raised his hands in a placating gesture. "It's not what you're thinking."

"Zoe?" Tiffany's voice came from the bottom of the stairs. She jogged up and stopped next to Orion. "I heard yelling. Are you okay?"

More footsteps and voices bore down on us. There was no way we were going to be able to keep the truth about Victoria's death a secret now.

"They think I hurt Victoria." Leo turned a pleading

gaze on Tiffany, as if somehow she'd be able to clear every-thing up for him even though I was the one who found him and Ryan was the one with the badge. "But I didn't. I swear I didn't."

Darcy pushed past Tiffany. "Does that mean her death wasn't an accident?"

Graudin joined Darcy on the landing. He pointed a thick finger at Ryan. "When were you going to tell us?"

Ryan's face stayed so calm I couldn't tell whether he was frustrated, annoyed, or thinking about something entirely different. He had to teach me how to do that. There had to be some trick to it. He didn't even engage in any of the self-protective gestures like crossing his arms that I might have instinctively defaulted to.

"Mr. Graudin," Ryan's voice was firm, "this is an active investigation. I'm under no obligation to reveal any of the details to you."

Graudin's chest puffed out. "I'd say you are when we're stuck here with a murderer."

Mason and Simone brought up the rear of the group, stopping a few steps down from the top.

Simone clutched her chihuahua to her chest. "What's going on?" Her voice still had an airy quality, and her eyes didn't seem quite focused. A sedative, maybe?

Tiffany reached out a hand as if she were looking for the railing to steady herself. She caught hold of my arm instead and didn't let go. "No one here could have killed Victoria. I'm sure no one here could have."

My chest went tight, and I rested my hand over

Tiffany's on my arm. The color had all gone out of her cheeks. All of a sudden, she looked thirteen instead of twenty. Why had I assumed this wouldn't bother her just because she wasn't afraid of a dead body? I should have asked Ryan if I could warn Tiffany at least. She certainly hadn't pushed Victoria down the stairs, regardless of Ryan's desire to suspect everyone. She was so tiny Victoria probably wouldn't have even felt it.

Darcy pursed her lips until they formed such a thin line that they almost disappeared. "Of course someone here could have killed her. Someone here must have. We're the only ones in the building. And it was probably someone who knew her already, instead of the janitor." She hooked a thumb at Leo. "Saying the janitor did it is like the modern version of saying the butler did it."

I smothered down a laugh. Not appropriate to laugh right now. But honestly, did she think this was some sort of Agatha Christie novel?

Darcy narrowed her eyes to match her lips and turned toward Mason. "You sure seemed cozy with her earlier. Maybe you tried something, she refused you, and you wanted to get even with her."

Mason raised his eyebrows. "Your evidence that I killed her is that I was nice to her? You and Victoria didn't have a civil word for each other all day. Every time she so much as looked in your direction, you snapped at her. That would seem to indicate guilt more so than my politeness."

Darcy drew back, and red blotches bloomed in her cheeks. "That doesn't mean I *killed* her. I'm not the one who was trying to flee during a blizzard." She directed a pointed gaze at Graudin. "I wasn't willing to risk my life to leave the scene."

"Don't pretend you didn't want to leave, too." Graudin's mouth turned down as if he'd just seen something disgusting. "I got kids at home waiting for me. That's not a crime. That's called responsible parenting."

I met Ryan's gaze around them. This was like dealing with squabbling kindergarteners. Except the kindergarteners would have been easier because at least I could have sent them to separate corners for a timeout.

"Enough." Ryan's voice cut through the noise, and Darcy and Graudin fell silent. "I'll be speaking to each of you. If you have any actual evidence to offer, that will be your opportunity."

"I saw him arguing with Victoria." Simone's tone swayed as if she weren't in complete control of it. "Would that be evidence?"

Everyone turned to look at her.

"You saw *who* arguing with Victoria?" Ryan asked.

She lifted a limp arm and point straight at Leo.

6

Ryan escorted everyone back to the convention hall and told them to stay there. Then he marched Leo back down the hallway to where Victoria's body lay under a sheet.

I trailed after them. Ryan glanced at me but didn't ask what I thought I was doing. Since he'd allowed me into the security room to watch the video footage with him, the command to stay in the convention hall surely didn't apply to me. Either that or he didn't want to argue with me in front of Leo.

A bead of sweat trickled down Leo's temple. He looked at the floor, the wall, the ceiling, everywhere other than at Victoria's body. Whether he was the killer or not, he wasn't a heartless killer. If he'd been the one to push Victoria down the stairs, he seemed to feel enough guilt now that he couldn't look at what he'd done.

Ryan didn't do anything without thinking it through

carefully. Questioning Leo near Victoria's body must be calculated to see how he'd react to her corpse.

Ryan pulled out his phone and opened the audio recording app. He listed all three of our names and the date. "Do you—"

Teddy's high-pitched barks cut off whatever Ryan had been about to say. That gave new meaning to the saying *Let sleeping dogs lie*. He'd been out so soundly that he hadn't realized we were there until Ryan spoke.

I pressed Orion's leash into Ryan's hand. "I'll find someone who can take care of Teddy while we talk."

Ryan leaned forward, as if he wasn't sure he'd heard me correctly. "Teddy?"

I shrugged. "I had to call him something other than *dog*."

I untied Teddy's leash. Bringing him close to Victoria's body obviously wasn't the solution to his barking that we'd been looking for. This had to be a case of poor socialization as a puppy.

Teddy trotted along beside me, keeping as much distance between us as I'd allow, barking the whole way.

Everyone was back in the convention hall, as Ryan had commanded, but they weren't playing cards this time. They'd staked out their individual spots, and no one seemed to want to get too close to anyone else.

One by one, each head turned to look at us. Teddy's barking made him impossible to ignore.

Mason sat closest to the door, leaning back in a chair, his long legs stretched out in front of him. He cut and shuf-

fled a deck of cards so fast they blurred, without even looking. As a long-time dog show judge and breeder, he
seemed like the best option to babysit Teddy while I talked
to Leo with Ryan.

I headed in his direction, and the cards stopped
moving. "Would you be able to watch him for me for a
little bit?"

Before we could get within ten feet of him, Mason
scrambled to his feet and backed away. "No, thank you."

No, thank you? It's not like I was offering him second
helpings of something.

Darcy's spine straightened, and she looked up from the
game of solitaire she'd been playing with another deck.
"What are you doing judging dog shows if you don't like
dogs? That seems hypocritical."

Mason smoothed down the front of his suit jacket and
tugged at the bottom hem as if that would get rid of the
wrinkles that had set in and make him seem more professional. "I love dogs. But I like my hearing better. That dog's
bark could double as a tornado siren."

The fact that we had to yell our conversation to be
heard made Mason's concern less petty and more common
sense.

"Oh for heaven's sake." Darcy swept the cards up from
the floor and shoved them back into the package. "Give
him to me. Simone and I will figure something out. She's a
former vet tech. She must know how to deal with barking
dogs." She snatched his leash from my hand. "You go help
your boyfriend."

I opened my mouth to say that Ryan wasn't my boyfriend. That I had a wonderful boyfriend who wasn't here today. And to tell her that, as a vet, I also knew how to deal with barking dogs. But by the time I could get my tongue to form all those words, Darcy was far enough away that she'd never hear me over Teddy's racket.

Mason stooped down and retrieved Darcy's deck of cards from the floor. "I guess she won't be needing these for a while."

He headed with them in Graudin's direction.

At least Teddy was taken care of. Who did the caring didn't much matter.

I speed-walked back to where Ryan and Leo waited and took Orion's leash back. Ryan had let Leo sit on the floor. Leo had pulled his knees up, crossed his arms over his knees, and rested his head on top of them. It was a posture of defeat. Not necessarily one of guilt, though. I'd often sat that way when I felt like the world was against me and there was nothing I could do to change what was coming next, especially as a teenager.

Ryan gave me a look that clearly said *Remember, I'll be the one asking the questions.*

I smiled innocently in response, which wasn't the same as making any promises. Because I might come up with an important question that he hadn't thought of, and he obviously wouldn't want me to stay quiet then.

Ryan leaned against the wall next to where Leo hunched. "Do you understand how it looks that you were trying to enter the security office, Mr. Cooper?"

Leo slowly lifted his head. His eyes were rimmed in red. "It looks like I was trying to destroy any evidence against me, but I wasn't."

"Then why don't you tell us what you were doing there."

Leo ran both hands over his head, as if he could wipe this whole mess away. "I was trying to check and see if something was caught on video, but not Victoria's death."

Ryan didn't say anything. Words itched to spill out of my mouth to fill the pause, but that was the point. People felt compelled to fill the silence. The person we wanted to talk was Leo, not me. Besides, if I overstepped, Ryan might not let me continue to listen in.

Leo squirmed slightly. He clearly knew he needed to say more if he wanted to satisfy Ryan. "She bribed me to let her into the convention center early, ahead of the other vendors." He held his hands out, palms up. "I didn't see the harm. I figured she was nervous and needed more time to set up or something."

A *but* basically hung in the air. Had that been all there was to it, Leo wouldn't have been worried about what the video caught. Their agreement would have simply looked like two people having a conversation. Even Victoria handing Leo money wouldn't necessarily have been suspicious. And since Leo knew the convention center had cameras, he probably also knew they didn't capture audio.

I glanced at Ryan to see if he was going to fill in the *but* to prompt Leo to continue. He leaned against the wall, his arms crossed, with an expression that said he didn't believe a word Leo was saying. Which didn't mean that he didn't believe Leo. As I'd learned the hard way, Ryan was good at making it seem like people needed to convince him of their innocence.

I couldn't stand it. "And were you wrong?"

Leo nodded and hung his head. "I think she must have wanted in so she could read the signs that laid out where all the other vendors were going to set up." He swallowed hard once, twice. "And then make a plan for sabotaging anyone who was a direct competitor. I had to help one of the other vendors get rid of all the product she'd brought because someone destroyed it. That wasn't what I agreed to. I didn't want anyone to get hurt like that."

His voice had a frantic note to it. He reached a hand toward his pocket.

"Stop." Ryan's own hand slid toward where he always wore his concealed weapon.

Leo flinched and froze. "I just want to show you the money she gave me."

Ryan's hand stayed in place. "Slowly. Use two fingers. Nothing more."

This was why Ryan needed to be in charge. I wouldn't have thought to give those instructions. Leo couldn't very well pull a weapon on Ryan if he was only using two fingers, but he could pull something light like money out of his pocket if he were telling the truth.

Leo shifted and carefully wiggled his thumb and pointer finger into his right pants pocket. He pulled out folded hundred-dollar bills. "She offered me three hundred dollars. Money's tight right now, so I took it. Once I figured out what she did, I tried to give it back, but she wouldn't take it. She said I couldn't tell anyone or I'd be fired for breaking the rules and taking a bribe. She said she'd be quiet about it as long as I was." His shoulders drooped. "That was probably the conversation the chihuahua lady saw. That's what I was trying to find on the recordings. I know I looked angry."

So when the police had reviewed the video footage in-depth, the way Ryan and I hadn't had the time to do, they might have seen a heated discussion between Leo and Victoria. He would have become the obvious suspect. Assuming it was captured on the recording at all, given how spotty coverage was outside of the convention hall proper.

The money suggested he was telling the truth, at least in part. He likely wouldn't normally carry three hundred dollars in cash on him. That didn't mean he hadn't killed Victoria, though. "Maybe you killed her because you didn't trust her to keep quiet."

Ryan shot me a *You're only here to listen* look. I pretended like I didn't see it. It wasn't like I could have communicated the thought to him telepathically, and the idea needed to be addressed.

Leo shook his head. "She couldn't tell anyone because what she did was worse, destroying property like that. A woman like her probably had plenty of other enemies who'd want her dead. I wouldn't kill anyone, even for something more than losing my job."

Ryan extended his phone, where he was recording the conversation, slightly closer to Leo. He hadn't changed anything else in his posture or expression, but a little fission of energy zinged down my arms.

"How did you know," Ryan's voice had taken on a quietly dangerous tone, "that her death wasn't accidental?"

7

I tensed. How had I missed that? If Leo believed Victoria's death to be accidental the way I originally had, he'd have had no reason to try to get rid of the footage of his argument with her.

Leo's eyebrows pulled in at the center, and the corners of his mouth turned down. "I didn't know. That's why I needed to check. No one would care about what else was on the tapes if she tripped. They wouldn't even watch them." He sounded genuinely confused about the potential implications of him even thinking the recording could make him look guilty. "But the cameras, they don't always cover all the stairs. What if you couldn't see she tripped? Then you'd only see me angry with her. That wouldn't look good for me."

Ryan started to ask another question, but my phone rang. Had Judith finally gotten my messages? I fished the phone out of my pocket.

Blocked ID.

Telemarketers normally had some sort of number shown. Blocked ID usually meant someone from Children's Services. A smile grew across my face, and I softly bit my lower lip. Maybe I'd get my Christmas wish after all and Harper and I would be able to meet before Christmas. Maybe, since I was her sister, they'd let her join me for Christmas Day. If she wanted to, of course.

I slid my gaze to Ryan and Leo. Ryan would catch me up on anything else later. If I missed this call, we might not have time to arrange anything before Christmas, with only two weeks left. And the last thing I wanted to do was continue the visits with Tonya that I'd traded for the information I needed to find Harper without actually getting to be with Harper.

I motioned to Ryan that I needed to take the call. He gave a *go ahead* nod like he thought I was asking permission.

I slid my finger across the screen. "Dr. Zoe Stephenson."

"Zoe, I don't want you to panic."

The voice of Tina Foster, Harper's social worker, had the unnaturally calm tone that said there absolutely was something to panic about. I used that voice when there was a possibility that the animal I was treating had a life-threatening condition, but it wasn't confirmed yet. But at least I knew better than to say *I don't want you to panic*. As soon as you said that to anyone, that's automatically what they'd do. You might as well say *Don't think about a pink spotted elephant wearing a tutu.*

My throat was raw, like I'd swallowed little chips of glass, and they'd scratched all the way down. "Why shouldn't I panic?" I forced my voice to stay as level as possible, but it still squeaked up on the end.

"We have a situation with Harper, but I'm sure it'll resolve itself shortly."

If she'd been in an accident, and I was trapped here... No, I needed to stay calm. Whatever this was, I couldn't help Harper if I panicked. Maybe it wasn't even anything serious. It could be that there was a mix up with our paperwork that could delay things. But would something that benign merit a call like this from Tina? Who right now I wanted to shake for being so vague. The woman had shown she cared about Harper, but she was not the most organized, in any capacity.

Deep breaths. No shouting at her to spit it out already. "Can you start from the beginning, please?"

"I got a call this morning from Harper's foster parents that she's disappeared. Some of her clothes and other belongings are gone, including her backpack, so they think she's run away."

My chest clenched, crushing my lungs. "How is this something that will resolve itself shortly?"

"Most teenagers who run away return home within a couple of days." Tina's voice was so calm she might have been telling me that it was supposed to rain for a couple of days but that it'd clear up soon.

I took back everything I'd ever said about her caring about Harper. No one could be that calm about her being missing and actually care. "But you don't know that Harper will. It's winter in Michigan. She could freeze to death on the streets before someone decides that she's not coming home. Is anyone even looking for her?"

"We've contacted the police." Tina's tone shifted slightly, to that attitude customer service people often took if you tried to call them on anything that was being done wrong. "There's nothing more we can actually do."

Nothing more they could do? If I was able to leave here right now, I'd be on the streets myself, calling out her name. I'd be showing up at the houses of every single one of her friends. I wouldn't be sitting warm and safe in my office, waiting for the police to find her—presumably after some imaginary time period had passed in which most teenagers returned home.

You need Tina on your side, a little voice in my head that sounded a lot like Judith said. *Don't alienate her.*

Why did even Judith's imaginary advice have to be so reasonable? Though that's why I valued her advice so much. Someone had to temper my tendency to, as our grandma liked to describe it, shoot first and ask questions after the bodies were cold.

I sucked in a long breath until I was sure I could speak without shouting. "Will you call me if there's any news?"

"Of course." The pleasant tone was back to her voice. "And really, this happens all the time. It's very rare that teens don't come back. I'm sure Harper will be home by Monday."

I disconnected the call and made a face at the phone, but it only made me feel marginally better. I slid it back in my pocket and turned in a slow circle. Even though I'd answered the call next to the stairway and Victoria's body, I'd somehow ended up past the convention hall. My frustration must have been coming out as speed walking, Orion trotting along beside me, and I hadn't even noticed. Now that we'd stopped, he plopped his bum down, his tongue lolling out.

I knelt down next to him, wrapped my arms around his neck, and buried my face in his fur. How could this be happening? This wasn't how it was supposed to go. Why would she run away now?

Tonya would say it was my fault. What would make me think Harper would want me as a sister? Running away would be better than having to put up with me.

Maybe Tonya had even planted that idea in Harper's head. I should have asked Tina if Harper had been to see our biological mother recently. What chance did I have if Tonya had poisoned Harper against me before we'd even met? It'd taken years for me to work through the lies she'd put in my head about my dad, and that had been while living with him and seeing a family counselor. Harper might never be able to sort out the truth from Tonya's lies if we didn't get enough time together.

"Zoe?" Tiffany's hesitant voice came from behind me. "Can I talk to you about something?"

I scrambled to my feet. At least I hadn't been crying. I wouldn't have been able to wipe tears away without Tiffany seeing. The last thing I wanted was to scare her. This place was a bowl full of tension already without me adding to it.

I swallowed hard and turned to face her. "Of course." I forced a bright tone into my voice. "What's up?"

She twisted her fingers together in front of her. "It's about Leo. I wanted to speak up for him."

Leo had looked at Tiffany when we'd found him outside the security office and he'd been pleading his innocence. He hadn't looked at anyone else that way. I knew something felt off about that. "Were you with him when Victoria fell down the stairs?"

I couldn't quite bring myself to say *when Victoria was killed*. I was probably projecting my feelings about Harper onto Tiffany, but I had this irrational urge to protect her as much as I could. She was so much closer in age to Harper than she was to me.

Tiffany shook her head. "I'm not sure exactly when that would have been, but I was either taking stuff out to my car or waiting with Orion in the convention hall." At his name, he perked his ears up as if Tiffany might be letting him know a treat was coming. "But I know him. From before. He used to work at my parents' funeral home."

Well, that explained why she didn't seem upset by a dead body. If she'd spent any time around her parents' business, she would have seen plenty of dead bodies.

Tiffany stepped forward, her hands slightly out front of herself as if pleading with me. "He wouldn't have hurt Victoria. He was always so good-natured, even when clients took their grief out on him."

But Leo worked here now. Not for her parents. If he'd been such a great employee, why wasn't he still working there? I couldn't say it that way, obviously. That would, as Judith would surely have told me, sounded confrontational. People were so much more complicated than animals.

Why doesn't he still work for your parents? Would that still sound accusatory?

Screw it. We were trying to solve a murder here. "Do you know why he stopped working for your parents?"

Tiffany didn't frown or scowl at me. She nodded emphatically. She really was almost ridiculously easy going. "It wasn't anything bad. His mom couldn't live on her own anymore, but she was refusing to leave her home. Leo and his wife moved in with her, and the commute was too far for him to drive to Arbor every day."

Money's tight right now, Leo had said. Presumably, if his mother wasn't able to live on her own anymore, she had medical conditions. Maybe expensive ones.

Leo's attempt to get into the security office made him look guilty, but I didn't think he'd killed Victoria. I couldn't prove it in any sense that would satisfy Ryan or anyone else on the police force. It was more like the same instinct that guided which direction I went to figure out a mysterious illness in a patient.

Even if Leo had lost his job working at the convention center, he wouldn't have been out of options. He could have gone back to work for Tiffany's family, even though the hour-long commute each way would have been difficult. At least he could have done that until he found another position closer. And based on what Tiffany said, her parents would have given Leo a glowing recommendation. He didn't need a reference from the conference center to find another job.

None of that added up to the picture of a man desperate enough to kill.

I'd have to tell Ryan everything Tiffany had said as soon as he finished with Leo.

A stuttering sensation filled my chest. Ryan might know what to do about Harper, too. I should have thought of that right away.

Tiffany was twisting her fingers together again. "Would you tell all that to Detective MacIntosh for me?"

Heaviness settled on my shoulders. Why *had* Tiffany come to me instead of going directly to Ryan? The only reason I could come up with was a bad one—she thought I'd be easier to manipulate. Though, her story would be a simple enough one for Ryan to check. One call to Tiffany's parents and another to Leo's wife would confirm or deny her story.

Ugg. The gears in my brain for suspicion and paranoia were starting to spin out of control—yet another lovely little gift Tonya left me. After a year working with a therapist in high school to recognize for myself when I might be making unwarranted assumptions about other people's motives and another year developing the courage to ask for clarification, shouldn't both come more naturally? Instead, they were like those piano lessons Judith and I had taken for a couple of years as kids. We'd make great progress as long as we were constantly practicing and then seem to lose most of it over the summer when we didn't have lessons.

I drew a slow breath. Life skills weren't something I could let slide like my abilities as a pianist. The consequences were bigger than not being able to accompany the singing in church. "Is there a reason you didn't want to tell Detective MacIntosh yourself?"

Tiffany blushed. "I know he's your friend and stuff, but he's a little scary. Especially when he scowls at you. I couldn't even handle it when a cop pulled me over to tell me I had a taillight out. I burst into tears thinking he was going to arrest me. If I try to talk to Detective MacIntosh, I'm going to trip over my words and make no sense."

I snorted. "He's going to love hearing that."

Tiffany blanched.

I held up my hands. "Kidding." I gave her a genuine smile this time. "I'll tell him what you said, but I promise I'll leave out the 'he's scary' part."

Tiffany let out a breath, and her body sagged. "Thanks. I'll see you back in the convention hall, okay? Simone said I could play with Lucy if I wanted."

She hurried off back down the hall.

All things considered, Tiffany was handling the situation really well. I'd have to suggest that Judith give her more responsibilities at the shelter.

I headed back to where I'd left Leo and Ryan. Leo sat with his head in his hands, while Ryan made notes in his notebook. He glanced up as I approached.

I waved for him to join me.

I power-walked down the hall. Ryan followed after me. I went thirty feet down the hall before stopping. Hopefully that would be far enough away that Leo wouldn't be able to hear us if we kept our voices down, but still close enough that Ryan could keep an eye on him.

Ryan drew up beside me. "If this is a very slow game of tag, I'm not sure I have the energy."

I put my back to Leo so that Ryan could talk to me while keeping Leo in sight. I filled him in on what Tiffany had told me, leaving out why she hadn't told him directly, the way I'd promised.

Ryan closed his eyes for a second and opened them again. "I think you're right. He wasn't smart, but he also probably isn't our killer. Which at least brings us down to five suspects."

"Four. Tiffany didn't do it, either."

Ryan rolled his eyes. "You know that you can't just eliminate someone as a suspect because you like them, right? How you feel about someone isn't evidence."

Not for him. But as he liked to tell me, I wasn't a police officer. I didn't have to follow the same rules. "You can keep her on your list if you'd like, but it's a waste of time. She didn't have time to tie Orion up somewhere, kill Victoria, and get back before I did."

Ryan made a huffing noise that I took as acquiesce. "Either way, I'm not going to let on that I think Leo is innocent. We lost our edge when everyone found out we knew it was a murder, but we can gain some of it back if they think we're focused on Leo and not looking at anyone else."

I nodded, but the words *not looking* brought Harper right back to the forefront of my mind. My throat tightened. Why would they not be actively looking for her? Did they think she wasn't worth it because she was a foster kid? Or because our bio mom was in prison? Tonya's reputation had certainly caused me enough trouble growing up. But Harper wasn't Tonya any more than I was Tonya. They shouldn't assume Harper had run away because Tonya was an addict and a murderer.

Ryan hunched down slightly, looking in my face. "What's wrong? Please tell me you didn't find another body." There was a teasing note to his words.

I glanced back at Leo. He didn't seem to be paying any attention to us, lost in his own worries. "The phone call I got earlier. It was about Harper." I recapped the conversation with Tina.

Ryan let out a long breath. "Okay. So, first, Harper's social worker was telling you the truth. Most runaway teenagers do come back home on their own within a couple of days. The situation is different than when a small child goes missing. That's often an abduction. But teens usually go missing because of a personal problem they don't know how to face. They come back as soon as they calm down."

"But what if she didn't run away?" My head spun like I was on one of those awful teacup rides at fairs that my dad loved. "What if someone took her?"

Ryan lifted his hands as if he wanted to place them on my upper arms to help hold me together. He let them fall back to his sides. "Is there a reason someone might take her?"

The spinning inside me slowed. He hadn't brushed off my concern. He was actually listening and considering it. I wasn't going to have to argue to get him to take me seriously.

I closed my eyes. For whatever reason, by listening, by not brushing me off, it was like he helped me look at my own fears more objectively. *Was* there a reason someone might take her? The fear had come out of me like a mudslide, all gut reactions. But Tonya wouldn't have the means or a reason to have Harper kidnapped. The only people I'd made angry enough to seek revenge were already in prison, and they wouldn't have known about Harper anyway. "It could have been a random kidnapper."

"Were there signs of a struggle?"

I shook my head. "Not according to Tina. Her foster parents said it looked like she'd packed some of her stuff."

"Then she probably left of her own free will." His deep voice had a soothing quality to it, and I breathed a little more deeply. "Tell me where Harper lives. I'll make a call to the closest station. As a professional courtesy, the officer who was assigned her case might tell me if Harper has a history of running away. If she does and she's always come back, then there's a good chance she'll return on her own again. If not, we'll make a plan to find her."

8

I headed back to the conventional hall. Ryan said he needed a few more minutes to decide how much to tell Leo. Did we let him keep thinking he was the main suspect, or did we ease his mind and ask him to play along? My vote had been to let Leo in on it. Putting him under the stress of continuing to believe he was suspected of murder seemed unkind. Ryan pointed out that Leo might not be a good actor.

The convention hall was quiet, as if everyone felt the need to whisper. Above, the heating vents rattled as they shot out warm air, probably the last for the night since we were getting close to when the thermostat would automatically lower and the lights would shut off. Chihuahua claws clicked on the tile floor as Tiffany threw a tiny stuffed dinosaur that Simone must have had tucked away somewhere for Lucy. Lucy picked it up and brought it back.

That was one benefit of a small dog. If I wanted to keep all of Orion's supplies with me, I'd need a steamer trunk.

Graudin had staked out his own corner. He must figure isolation and boredom were better than associating with a potential murderer. Either that or he was the murderer and he thought he'd look less suspicious by acting suspicious of everyone else. The possibilities made my head ache.

Darcy and Mason sat a little way from Tiffany. Mason was making a coin disappear and reappear for her. Simone sat nearby. She still didn't look entirely lucid, but at least she was sitting up on her own and trying to pay attention to what Mason was doing. That was an improvement. Thank goodness Mason was here and willing to provide a distraction for them. The tension had seemed to be growing for the past few hours. Everyone needed something other than murder and death to focus on. Mason's voice carried softly, with the kind of misdirection talk that all people who did magic tricks seemed to default to.

I glanced around. Why was it so quiet? I shouldn't have been able to hear anything over Teddy's barking, let alone soft speech. Had Darcy or Simone gotten tired of Teddy's barking and locked him in a closet? We were going to have words if they had.

I turned in a circle. Teddy rested peacefully in a crate on the far side of the hall, right next to the other set of doors.

Simone was officially a genius.

I hurried over to her. "Did he quiet down as soon as you crated him?"

"Hmmm?" Simone glanced away from Mason's trick, then over at Teddy. "Oh. No. He still barks whenever someone gets close to him. The crate just keeps him safe and away from everyone so he stays quiet." Her voice sounded airy, like someone blowing sound across a pop-bottle top. "I noticed that was how Victoria was keeping him quiet during the event, and Darcy saw his crate was still there and set up when she and Tiffany counted the dog meals. They carried it to a spot far away from the rest of us." She fluttered a hand in the air. "I would have helped, but I'm not feeling steady on my feet right now."

No one else had thought to crate him, not even me. Hadn't Darcy said Simone used to be a vet tech? If she was still licensed, maybe she'd consider coming to work for Maeve and me at the clinic. We could use someone with experience and creative thinking. April was so newly grad-uated that I often ended up feeling like a babysitter rather than a boss. And one vet tech wasn't nearly enough. We needed another vet, and at least two more techs with the way our practice was growing. Simone might finally be a step toward solving one of those problems. If she was this creative when she'd taken something to ease her anxiety, I could only imagine how she'd be normally.

Assuming she wasn't the killer. No one else had paid enough attention to Victoria during the day to know what she did with Teddy to keep him from barking the whole time. That made her either observant or otherwise motivated.

I wouldn't get answers by staring at her.

I sat cross-legged on the floor next to her. "Darcy mentioned you used to be a vet tech. Have you ever thought about going back to it? My clinic might be hiring in the near future."

Technically, we were hiring now, but Maeve wouldn't be happy with me if I practically offered the job to someone she'd never met, who might or might not be a murderer. Simone seemed to be struggling with what happened to Victoria more than anyone else, if the pills she was taking were any indication. That could point to a guilty conscience.

Simone made a small huffing sound. "I can't go back. It was too much."

I didn't have to ask why. She didn't need to explain. You got into a career as a veterinarian or a veterinary technician because you loved animals, and you quickly found out that it was one of the most difficult jobs for someone who loved animals. The thing you most needed—compassion for your patients and their families—was also what would burn you out and use you up if you weren't careful. Sometimes even if you were.

She sighed softly. "That's why I was trying to start a gourmet dog biscuit company. Baking was supposed to be soothing."

Trying to start. *Supposed* to be. That sounded like it wasn't going very well. Perhaps she and Victoria had been competing, and Victoria was cutting too far into Simone's profits. That could be motive for murder. Whoever pushed Victoria down the stairs had to have a reason for doing it. Unless someone was mentally unstable, they didn't go pushing random people down the stairs for no reason. If I could find a motive, that might help us narrow down our suspect pool even further.

I needed to find out if she and Victoria had met before and could have had a history. "Was this your first event?"

"First, and last." Simone's gaze wandered away from mine to land on Lucy wrestling with her dinosaur on the floor. "I didn't realize how easily something could happen to my product. It hasn't been a great day all around."

That's right. Simone had been the one who said her entire inventory was destroyed before the event got started. "What happened to your product?"

She pulled her orange pill bottle out of her purse and passed it back and forth between her hands as if she were considering taking another one. She shrugged slowly. "The booth next to me had one of those water cooler-sized thermos things full of hot chocolate. It tipped over onto my biscuits, and then I couldn't sell them. They said it wasn't even theirs when I asked, but I think they just didn't want to have to pay for what got ruined."

I barely stopped myself from sucking in a breath. Leo had confronted Victoria because he figured out she wanted into the building early to sabotage direct competitors. With that extra time, she could have planned a way to make sure no one purchased Simone's biscuits over her meals. For all we knew, Victoria hadn't simply set it up. She could also have been the one to "accidentally" knock it over.

Simone seemed a little fragile to begin with. Could that have pushed her over the edge?

Not exactly proof, but it was more than I'd had a few minutes ago. Enough to bring to Ryan at least. I just couldn't let her know I suspected. "I'm sorry that happened."

Simone shrugged again. "Things happen. You learn from them and move on."

I got up and dusted off the back of my jeans. "Time to feed Orion and find a place for us to bed down for the night."

Simone nodded vaguely, even though it was still early enough that most toddlers wouldn't be asleep yet. It wasn't entirely an excuse to escape. I didn't want to be stumbling around this place after the lights went out with only a flashlight to guide me. That'd be too eerie, especially with how the wind outside kept battering the building and making it groan as if it were alive.

I fed Orion and then got another meal for Teddy. Even though I worked as quickly as possible to feed Teddy and flee the bark zone, by the time I finished, my ear rang. When I got back to Orion, he was already licking his empty bowl as if that would make more food magically appear.

Leo came in the doors nearest to Teddy, with Ryan close behind him. As soon as Leo got within ten feet of the crate, Teddy forgot his food. His front legs popped off the floor with every bark, as if he were throwing his whole body into it to get as much volume as possible.

If I didn't know that he reacted that way to everyone, I would have assumed he was trying to tell us that Leo was the one who pushed Victoria down the stairs. But that couldn't be the case, otherwise Ryan and I would also be implicated as Victoria's murderers.

Orion huffed softly behind me and laid down with his back to Teddy's crate as if even he was tired of the racket. Not even continuing to lick the food bowl could make up for it.

Ryan grabbed a chair and ushered Leo to the corner of the room opposite Teddy's crate, farthest from the doors. "I need everyone's attention."

As if we were all puppets and he held the strings, all the heads in the room swiveled toward him. What would this have been like if he hadn't still been here? A shiver skittered along my skin like a spider scurrying down a wall. Without him, I wouldn't have known what to do about Victoria's body. I wouldn't have been able to get into the security office to keep the recording of Victoria's fall from being recorded over. And who knew what everyone would have done without Ryan standing in a position of authority for them to listen to and follow? We could have had a modern-day version of *Lord of the Flies*.

"Mr. Cooper isn't supposed to leave this room unless I'm with him," Ryan said. "If he tries, someone should find me immediately. He's agreed to this, and this isn't a statement of his guilt or innocence."

Graudin snorted. Normally it probably wouldn't have been loud enough for the rest of us to hear, but with Teddy and everyone else quiet, he might as well have shouted.

Darcy glared at him.

Graudin shrugged. "What? It's not like everyone else wasn't thinking the same thing."

She flipped him the middle finger.

Ryan cleared his throat. Like two naughty students caught poking each other, Darcy and Graudin quieted again. "I'll be sleeping in the hallway to keep Victoria's body secure. While I can't force you to do what I say, I'd ask that the rest of you not leave this room until morning."

Graudin pointed at Leo. "How do we know he won't sneak away while we're all asleep?"

I barely stopped myself from rolling my eyes. Leo hadn't moved from where Ryan had placed him earlier, even when I'd pulled Ryan away to talk. Was it awful of me to hope Graudin was the killer instead of Simone? The man was horrible.

Ryan nodded at Graudin, giving the question more legitimacy than I'd been willing to extend. "I'm asking for volunteers to each take a turn sitting up to watch him. You can decide the order among yourselves, but the easiest way would be to go alphabetically."

Tiffany picked up Lucy's dinosaur and tucked it back into Simone's oversized bag. "Can't the cameras just watch him?"

Everyone's gazes snapped to her.

Mason frowned. "What are you talking about?"

Tiffany pointed up toward the corner of the ceiling. The camera blended in unless you looked right at it. Even I'd overlooked them, and I knew they were there.

Tiffany lowered her arm. "The cameras. Though I guess that would only show the police when he'd left. It wouldn't stop him from leaving." She glanced at Leo and gave him a tentative smile. "Not that I think he's going to try."

"There are more than one?" Darcy rotated slowly in a circle, her face turned upward, almost identically mimicking what I'd done earlier when I'd learned about them. "Are they in the hallways as well?"

Graudin sniffed loudly enough for everyone to hear it. "We can't stay here with cameras recording our every move. There's no privacy. That has to be against the law."

"There's no reason you should have a problem with video cameras unless you're planning on doing something you shouldn't," Leo said softly from his chair. "Believe me."

If anyone would know the truth of that, it was Leo. We'd never have found out about his deal with Victoria if he hadn't panicked and tried to access the security office to erase the evidence of it.

Graudin stiffened and crossed his arms over his chest. "Not that it's any of your business, but I don't like to sleep fully clothed. It's too restrictive."

Tiffany and Simone both gasped, while Darcy shook her head.

Mason swore—and not softly. "You need to keep your clothes on. All of them."

"I agree," Tiffany said.

Graudin's face turned an unnatural shade of pastel red. "This is still a free country, last I checked."

"Enough." Ryan held up his hand. "I've already turned the cameras off, but this is a public space, so anyone who doesn't want to be charged with indecent exposure will be keeping all their clothes on. Is that understood?"

Graudin scowled but finally nodded.

"It'll be cold enough soon that everyone will want as many layers as they can get, anyway," Leo said.

Graudin turned his glare on Leo, then flopped down onto his stack of bedding, mostly a ratty plaid blanket and a summer coat that must have been stuffed in the back of his truck from warmer weather. "I'll take the first watch. Since we've been told it's alphabetical—" He shot a look at Ryan that would have flayed anyone else's skin off. "—and my last name begins with a G."

Darcy kept glancing up at the cameras. "What if we need to use the bathroom in the night? Those are in the hallway."

A slightly crazy laugh bubbled up inside me. I stuffed it back down. Forget kindergarteners, this must be what it's like to be a counselor at a summer camp. The rowdy behavior of little kids, plus talking back.

Ryan pulled a notebook from his pocket and wrote something down. He ripped the paper out and placed it on the table nearest the door. "That's my cell number and

Zoe's cell number. You can call one of us, and I'll come escort you to the bathroom."

Simone blinked at him as if the words were taking a while to register. "Where will Zoe be?"

Darcy rolled her eyes as if that were obvious. Glad she thought so, since I hadn't even figured it out yet.

"With me," Ryan said. "If I need to escort one of you, she'll watch the body."

9

I peeked at Ryan out of the corner of my eye as we walked with Orion back toward Victoria's body. I had Orion's leash looped over my arm and my hands full of a paper plate with two burgers that Tiffany had cooked for supper and saved for us, plus two bottles of water. "For someone who was giving me a hard time earlier today about how I'm not a police officer, you didn't waste any time assigning me to guard Victoria's body."

Ryan shifted my bedding in his arms for a more secure hold. "You're the only one I can be sure isn't a murderer."

An image of him sitting across from me in the police station, trying to trick me into confessing to murdering Sebastian Clunes, flashed across my mind. "I bet you never thought you'd be saying those words when we first met." I let a teasing note steal into my voice so he'd know I wasn't still angry with him. "How can you be sure this time that I'm innocent? I don't have an alibi."

Ryan lowered his chin and raised his eyebrows in a look that clearly said *Are you serious?* "I also didn't want to risk you sleeping in the same room as whoever actually did kill Victoria. You have a way of making yourself the target of killers."

I elbowed him in the ribs, and he let out a soft *oof*, followed by a chuckle. Just because he was right didn't mean he needed to rub it in. I filled him in on what I'd learned from Simone. "Was there anything helpful in Victoria's call history?"

Ryan shook his head. "No last names match anyone here. Frankel even checked back a year in case she had a pattern of dating married men. She seemed to break off a relationship with a man named Glen Hartford a few months ago. Her current boyfriend, Timothy Van, gave him the name of Victoria's mother. Frankel's notifying her. He's going to see if her family recognizes the names of anyone here or knows of anyone else she might have been seeing. We have no reason to think she was monogamous in her adulterous relationships."

We reached the spot near Victoria's body where Ryan had already set up his own bedding. We weren't as close to Victoria's body as I'd been expecting, but that had to be for the best. Even at this distance, I could smell the odors that came with death. It'd only get worse the longer we were trapped here.

Ryan laid out my bedding a respectable five feet from his.

While he was doing that, I pulled out my phone and

tried Judith again. No answer.

I dialed Keith's number. "Have you heard anything from Judith?" I asked as soon as the hellos were out of the way.

"She and Bob made it back safely. The roads were so bad they had to drive twenty miles per hour the whole way. It took them hours."

I pressed a hand to my throat and sent up a prayer of thanks. No wonder she hadn't been home when I thought she should. "Did she say anything about why she wasn't answering her phone?"

"Ran out of battery, and the landlines are down all over town. Apparently, one of the main lines iced over and snapped. Judith's planning to stay at the shelter tonight to make sure the generator doesn't go out. She wanted you to know that she'll charge her phone while she's there. If Ryan wants them to feed his cats and dog, he needs to text Bob where he can find a spare key."

Keith sounded like he was repeating a script.

"Did she write that down for you?"

Keith chuckled. "She said it wasn't that she didn't trust me. She just knew how worried you'd be, and she wanted to make sure I had all the answers to your questions."

My throat tightened slightly. What I wouldn't give to be at home with Judith right now drinking hot chocolate and having her talk me out of any schemes for finding Harper that were too crazy. "Thanks. I'll call you tomorrow once I know when we might be able to leave here."

I disconnected the call.

The lights snapped off around me, throwing the hallway into darkness. Small emergency lights glowed at regular intervals along the ceiling. Leo had been telling the truth about the convention center's systems being on a timer, if nothing else.

I switched on the flashlight on my phone and picked my way over to where Ryan and Orion had already bedded down. I squinted. A sleeping bag and travel pillow lay where my cobbled-together bedding should be. Orion lay on the blanket I'd had for him in the back seat of my car. Ryan had removed his suit jacket and was bundling it up to form a makeshift pillow. He slid his winter coat back on. He sat on the meager bedding that was supposed to be mine—a couple of towels that no doubt smelled like dog, an extra blanket Tiffany had in her car, and the shiny emergency rescue blanket I kept in my trunk.

"I didn't have a sleeping bag in my car." The words were out before I could stop to consider how stupid they sounded. The sleeping bag was clearly his, and he'd given it to me. Heat scorched my neck and into my cheeks. I turned off my phone light and sat. "Thank you. This should be yours."

I couldn't see him, but there was the rustle of fabric shifting around. "For a woman who likes to be prepared, I was surprised you didn't have one of your own. Once we get out of this, I'm taking you to the store to put together a better winter car kit."

Glare at him or thank him? Orion rolled over slightly, legs in the air and belly up. I rubbed his tummy. I let the moment pass. Best not to tick off the man who gave me the more comfortable sleeping setup.

I took off my coat and tossed it over to Ryan. Thanks to his sleeping bag, I should be warm enough without it. I told him about Bob's offer, and the clicking noises of him writing a text trickled over to me.

"You didn't tell Keith about Harper." Ryan's voice came from floor level, as if he'd laid down.

I crawled into the sleeping bag and draped an arm over my eyes. Of course he'd notice. He seemed to notice everything. Especially the things I didn't want him to. "Keith and I aren't in agreement about Harper. I want Harper to live with me. Keith thinks she should stay with her foster family." Balls of tension formed at my temples, and my stomach knotted. Keith had been so adamant when I'd told him what I wanted to do. He'd had so many objections. "He wants to have kids as soon as we get married. What if Harper would be a danger to our kids? And he wants to go back into the military. Wouldn't it be too much for me to handle a troubled teenager and small children if he gets deployed again?"

My back muscles hardened into concrete as I repeated Keith's questions. I didn't have answers for him. Which was probably why I'd been avoiding continuing the conversation. And sometimes it felt like he didn't really want answers. He just wanted me to agree with him.

"Does that mean you've decided to get married?" Ryan's voice had a strange rasp to it that hadn't been there before. "I didn't see a ring."

Orion shifted so that his head rested on my chest, his body curled into mine for warmth. "Keith hasn't officially proposed yet, but he's talked about it."

"*He's* talked about it." Ryan's voice went up at the end, making it almost a question, but not quite.

Was this a detective thing, this ability to pick up on nuances and word choices? Since he was going to hear everything I didn't say, I might as well admit to all of it.

I rolled toward him, even though I couldn't see him past Orion's bulk. I draped an arm across Orion, and he sighed. "Keith's sure about us getting married, but I'm not."

I cringed. That sounded worse out loud than I thought it would. Who didn't know how they felt about someone after eight months together?

A rolling pressure built inside my chest. What if it wasn't that I didn't know? Because I *did* know what kept pulling me back from making a full commitment. Could you care about someone and still not want to stay with them? "We seem to be at odds over a lot of things. Not just Harper. I want a houseful of pets, and he doesn't because he wants the freedom to move around. Maybe even overseas. But I don't want to move around all the time. I know home isn't about a place. It's about the people you're with. But that's just it. If we're always moving around, I won't be with anyone I love other than our little family unit. I want my kids to know their grandparents. I want my kids to play with their cousins. I want the kind of friendships that last so long they're more like family. I need that."

Tonya had dragged us from place to place every time a

landlord threatened to evict us if she didn't pay our overdue rent. Nothing had been stable.

And as living isolated in the city the past few years had shown me, I didn't do well on my own. I needed people around me who I trusted enough to talk to, so they could hold me accountable. Alone, it was too easy for me to rationalize anything.

"Have you said all this to Keith?" Ryan asked.

And there was the real problem. The reason I didn't want to continue having the same conversation over and over again. "I've tried. I don't think he heard me. It seems like he thinks I'll change my mind once we're married. But Judith and my parents love him. We share the same beliefs. He's hardworking and honest. He's loyal. He's kind. That should be enough, shouldn't it?"

Ryan didn't answer. I propped my chin on Orion's side so I could see him. He lay on his back, his head cradled in his hands, staring resolutely at the ceiling. Whether it was the dark or his training, his expression was completely unreadable.

I continued to stare at him until he glanced my way.

He sighed softly. "I'm not the right person for you to ask about this."

That was ludicrous. Just because he was single didn't mean he couldn't give me good advice. "I'd really appreciate your thoughts on it. You're more objective than Judith."

Ryan opened his mouth as if he were going to say

something, then closed it again. He scrubbed a hand over the stubble that'd started to darken his cheeks.

"You didn't say you loved him. You said Judith and your parents love him. But they're not the ones who'd be marrying him." His voice was cautious, his words slow, as if he were choosing them carefully. "You can't marry someone just to make your family happy. They wouldn't want that. I'm sure Keith doesn't want that to be the reason you marry him. It's not enough to base a lifetime on."

A picture of Judith and Bob sharing their Saturday morning breakfast popped into my mind. When they got married next year, Judith would be marrying her best friend. Whenever anything happened, it was always *I have to tell Bob*. When she wasn't sure what to do, it was *I'll ask Bob*. The picture they were painting of their future fit on the same canvas. Not like Keith and me, who kept stealing paints and brushes from each other, each trying to work on something separate, both wanting our picture to take priority.

But Judith wasn't me. Who wouldn't love Judith? She was everything I wanted to be and couldn't achieve. "It's not that simple." The admission stuck in my throat, but I pushed it free. I was never going to have the courage to admit this to someone in the daylight. "Keith loves me, and I'm not exactly easy to love. He's been willing to overlook a lot."

Tonya had made sure I knew that truth about myself from the moment I could walk and talk. I hadn't asked Keith to come with me on one of my monthly visitations to her yet, even though she'd been asking about my love life. I didn't need her driving home to him what was already obvious. I know what she'd say about the situation. *You're lucky anyone would want you. You're getting the better end of the deal here. He's going to have to put up with a lot.*

"Overlook a—" Ryan cut himself off. His tone was sharp. He sucked in a long breath.

I frowned. Was he upset? That made no sense. He of all people should understand what I meant. "You get it. I know I drive you crazy, too."

He rolled onto his side. His gaze on my face was intense even in the dim lighting. "Everyone has things about them that will drive you crazy. That's not the point. You should marry someone who sees you the way you are, good and bad, and who's still awed by you. He should feel like he doesn't deserve you. He should feel like he's a better man because of you. Because you make his life better. Because you make him look at his own flaws and want to be better."

Ryan's words wrapped around my heart and left a warm spot there. I broke his gaze and buried my face in Orion's neck. Did Keith feel like I made his life better? It didn't seem like it. It seemed like I was always doing something that wasn't quite right just by being me. He was always wishing I'd done something differently or said something differently, and he couldn't understand why I couldn't get it right. But he wanted to get married, and so he kept trying to make me fit the image of what he wanted. He didn't see *me*. Maybe he never had. Maybe what he loved was the image he'd created of me in his mind rather than who I really was.

And I'd been letting him get away with that out of fear that I'd never find someone who actually loved me for me. I'd been considering marrying him even though what we wanted out of life would never match. We could make that kind of marriage work if we were committed to it, but it'd never be as fulfilling as the kind of marriage Judith and Bob would have or the kind of marriage my dad and Camille had.

Keith and I weren't better together than we were apart.

"I'm not that for him." I couldn't look at Ryan as I said it. It was too humiliating that I'd let my relationship with Keith go on this long when deep down some part of me always knew it wasn't working. "He's not that for me, either."

"Then you need to tell him that. It's kinder to be honest with him."

World's worst timing. I didn't want to be the jerk who broke up with someone during the holidays.

My hands trembled. I was really going to end things. *Was* I really going to end things? "I'm scared."

I whispered the words. Ryan must have heard me because he slid his hand across Orion and into mine and gave it a quick squeeze.

"I know, but like I keep telling you, you're one of the bravest people I know."

10

I opened my eyes to Orion panting in my face. The hallway lights were back on. When had I fallen asleep? The last thing I remembered, Ryan and I were playing a game of *Would You Rather?* and I'd asked him if he'd rather be able to fly or breathe underwater.

What time was it? I reached for my phone and pressed my thumb to the home button. My phone didn't turn on. Ugg. I should have turned it off last night. Instead, I'd managed to run down the battery. I had a charger in the car, but it was meant to plug into the car, not a wall outlet. Would it even charge if I plugged it in when the car was off?

Orion whined softly. He probably needed a bathroom break, and he'd certainly want some breakfast. I sat up and rubbed sleep out of my eyes. Ryan was still sleeping. His phone rested near his head, a cord stretching back to the nearest outlet.

Surely he wouldn't mind if I unplugged his and plugged mine in. No need to wake him. I crawled out of the sleeping bag and shivered. The lights might be back on, but the building definitely hadn't warmed up yet, and Ryan was wrapped up in both our coats. I'd have to tough it out with just my sweater until he woke up.

I pulled my boots on, then crawled over to Ryan's phone. The gel he usually used to hold his curls in place had softened during the night, and his scruff from the day before had turned into the beginning of a beard. He looked good when he wasn't as formal.

Orion whined again, and heat blistered into my cheeks. The last thing I needed was for Ryan to wake up right now and find me staring at him. Talk about being creepy and awkward.

I quickly unplugged his phone and plugged mine in. I left his right next to mine so he wouldn't think someone had taken his for nefarious purposes.

Even with no coat, I didn't have a choice about where we went next. Not unless I wanted to ask Leo where I could find a mop and a bucket. Orion and I headed out into the cold.

The whiteness of it seared my eyeballs. The cars and trees were covered so only hints of color peeked out, a sliver of green here, a glimmer of blue and red there. The air smelled moist and bright rather than sharp and cold the way it had yesterday. Maybe that meant we were nearing the end of the storm. The snow was still coming down, though more lightly. If we got out of here today, it wouldn't be until much later in the afternoon, but at least there was hope.

Orion took care of his needs, and we headed back inside, my teeth chattering. I grabbed Orion's breakfast from the fridge in the cafeteria and carried it to the conventional hall where I'd left the bowls the night before.

Darcy, Graudin, Mason, and Leo appeared to still be asleep, but Simone and Tiffany were awake. They were taking turns throwing a miniature tennis ball for Lucy. Her tiny claws clicked across the floor with a skittering sound that made me think of robot crabs.

Orion squeaked and pulled slightly on his leash. Poor guy never seemed to figure out that small dogs were intimidated by him and didn't want to be his friend.

I wiggled the package of food, and his gaze snapped to it like Lucy didn't even exist. I picked up the bowl he'd used the day before and headed for a table. Tiffany got up and followed me.

She had that uncertain look on her face. Again. She was starting to remind me of April, seeking me out like a kitten after a mother cat. Was I this uncertain as a young adult? I smirked inside. I wasn't. I was worse. I acted like I knew everything and had all the answers. Judith was more like April and Tiffany.

I ripped open the package of food.

She reached my side. Her ponytail hung loose, her hair mussed on one side. She clearly hadn't been up long. "Zoe? Could I talk to you privately for a minute?"

Did she think I'd forgotten what she'd said earlier

about Leo because he was still being watched? "I told Ryan what you said. He has to follow protocol, but I don't think he suspects Leo anymore."

Tiffany shook her head. "I trust you. It's not about that."

Okay. Something new. Great. This was the weekend that would never end. "About Victoria's death? Because you really can talk directly to Ryan—Detective MacIntosh. He'll listen, and he's actually very kind."

"I can't tell him this." She'd dropped her voice to a whisper.

Tiffany peeked around me. I glanced back. No one else was anywhere near us.

Orion stuck his nose in my empty hand. His tongue came out and licked my palm.

"I don't want anyone getting in trouble." Tiffany's voice tugged my focus back to her. I practically had to watch her lips she was speaking so softly. Tiffany pulled out her hair tie, smoothed her hair, and tucked it back up again. "I don't know what the rules are around pills and stuff. But I think Simone's taking too many. I'm worried she's going to hurt herself."

I let out a slow puff of air. I'd been too distracted. Simone obviously hadn't been acting normally. She'd clearly been taking something to deal with the nerves and stress. But with everything else going on, I hadn't given more than a passing thought to whether she'd overdone it. If she overdosed, we had no way to get her help. And I did not relish the idea of sticking my fingers down her throat to make her vomit.

Orion shoved my hand harder. I moved to stroke his head, but he squirmed. "It's not illegal to take too many pills that have been prescribed to you. As long as you're not intending to harm yourself. It's stupid, but it's not illegal."

Tiffany flinched, like she might be reconsidering having me speak to Simone after all. Judith was the gentle one. I was the one who took a sledgehammer to things. She probably didn't realize that. She'd spent more time with Judith, and the easy assumption was that sisters would be more alike.

The packaged dog meal jerked in my grip. My gaze dropped. Orion had the corner in his teeth. He didn't let go when I looked at him. His expression said, *You clearly weren't going to feed me, so I had to fend for myself.*

I gave him my sternest look. "Drop it."

He hesitated for a fraction of a second, then his jaws opened just enough for the package to slip from his lips. He looked up at me with big, pleading eyes.

I poured it into the dish and set it on the floor for him. If I made him wait any longer, he'd be up on the table next. "Have you already talked to her and she wouldn't listen?"

Tiffany squished her lips together and shook her head. "Why would she listen to me? But she will if you talk to her. You're a doctor."

"I'm a veterinarian. Not the same thing."

Tiffany clasped her hands together and tucked them

into her stomach. "You know about drugs. You know the importance of proper doses and stuff. Would you talk to her? Please?"

Well, I certainly wasn't going to say no. If I didn't talk to Simone and she poisoned herself accidentally, I'd be partially responsible if I said nothing. I sighed and nodded.

I looked down at Orion. He'd laid down and tipped the bowl partway up with a single paw. I handed his leash to Tiffany and went back to the cafeteria for another portion of dog food to take with me to Simone for Lucy.

By the time I got back, both Graudin and Mason were up. Graudin, it appeared, had taken Ryan seriously and slept fully clothed, including his boots and his winter hat. Leo still lay on his bedding, his back to the room. The man was apparently a heavy sleeper.

I sat down next to Simone and handed her the package of food and a dog bowl. "Has Lucy eaten yet?"

She set the bowl aside and tore the package open. Lucy danced in front of her. "Not yet."

Her voice wasn't airy and disconnected anymore. Instead, she sounded like each word was dragging out of her painfully, the way my college roommate sounded the morning after she'd been out drinking. Tiffany was right. Whatever she'd taken yesterday had crossed the line of reasonable. She shouldn't be hung over.

I licked my lips. My instinct was to demand *How many pills have you taken? Give the rest to me.* Judith would surely tell me that wasn't the way to handle it. So what would she or our mom do?

I shifted uncomfortably. "How are you feeling this morning?"

Simone started to shake her head then stopped as if even that hurt. She pulled a chunk of meat from the food package and fed it to Lucy by hand as if she were a baby bird.

What was she doing? I'd brought her a bowl. It was sitting right there. Was she high right now?

"My head." Simone pulled another bit of something that looked like cooked carrot from the package. It dripped juice on the floor. Lucy snatched it from her fingers, then went after the droplets of gravy. "Is splitting open."

She scooped out a glob of something, and this time Lucy slurped it off her fingers. I gagged slightly. Seriously. She couldn't feed her that way at home all the time, could she?

With her non-gloop-covered hand, she fished around in her purse and pulled out her pill bottle. She wedged it between her knees and worked at the cap. The child-proof lid held fast.

I nodded toward the bottle. "Are those for headaches?"

Simone stuck her hand back into the food pouch. "Anxiety." The look she shot me said she dared me to say she didn't need them after everything that had happened.

I wasn't going to say she didn't need them. She might very well need them. All I was questioning was the quantity. "It's easy to take too many if you're not careful, and we're out here with no access to an ambulance if anything happens."

"I'm careful." Simone pressed down hard on the bottle and twisted. The top finally popped off. She reached her clean hand in and froze. She pulled it back out and lifted the bottle up to her face. "Oh. I could have..."

I leaned closer. The bottle only had two pills left inside.

She met my gaze. "You might be right." She twisted the lid back on. Her hand shook as she did it. She slowly held them out to me. I took the bottle from her.

"Zoe?" Tiffany called.

Do not snap at her, I silently admonished myself. *Even though she's interrupting you from doing what she asked you to do.*

I swiveled around. Tiffany held her phone up with one hand. "It's Judith for you. You weren't answering your phone."

I gave Simone's arm a quick squeeze and clambered to my feet.

I jogged to Tiffany and made a gimme-gimme gesture for the phone. I couldn't help myself. "My phone's dead. I don't even have it on me."

Tiffany handed the phone over.

"I don't have long," Judith said as soon as I answered. Cats meowed and dogs barked and whined in the background. She must be at the shelter, trying to care for all the animals herself or with only Bob for help. "But I wanted to make sure you were okay."

Was I okay? A lump formed in my throat. I was trapped

in a building with a dead body and a murderer. Harper was missing. And I was planning to break up with my boyfriend. I was a lot of things, but *okay* probably didn't make the top five.

I opened my mouth to tell her I was fine, so that she didn't worry. The news about Harper spilled out instead. "Ryan has a call it to the station handling her disappearance, but there's nothing else we can do right now."

"I'm so sorry. I'll be praying for her to be found safe." There was a rattling sound like she was filling a dog dish with kibble. "I'm surprised Keith didn't tell me when I talked to him."

Oops. I'd walked straight into that one. "I didn't tell him. I..." Would it be easier or harder to tell Judith over the phone? I could use the excuse that I didn't want to hold her up since she was so busy. But at least over the phone I wouldn't have to see her disappointed face. "I had a long talk with Ryan last night, and I don't think Keith and I are going to work out."

Only background noise filled Judith's end as if she'd stopped moving. I held my breath.

Water ran on her end. "Did Ryan ask you to break up with Keith?" Judith's words were slow, as if she was choosing them carefully.

I squinched up my lips. What a silly question. "Of course not. He just helped me work through some things."

"Okay." Judith was still speaking slowly the way she did when she wanted to buy herself time to think about her words before she let them escape. "Well, I think you should wait until after the holidays before you make any decisions. He's eating Christmas dinner with us, and you're supposed to go with him to Ellery's New Year's Eve party. It wouldn't be right to break up with him until after that anyway."

I saw her point. I'd been worried because breaking up with someone over the holidays felt cruel, but it went beyond that. If I broke up with him immediately, he either wouldn't have anywhere to spend the holidays or we'd have to spend it awkwardly together regardless. "I'm not going to change my mind because I wait, though. Wouldn't I be leading him on if I wait?"

Judith spoke to one of the dogs, her voice distant like she'd pulled the phone away from her face for a minute. "If you had feelings for someone else, it'd be one thing. If you're just not sure yet about Keith, then give it more time. You haven't even known each other a year, and you've been commitment-shy since Sebastian. Don't do something you'll regret later."

I leaned back against the wall. Was that what was happening? Everything had seemed so clear when I talked to Ryan about it last night. The way he described what love should be like. I wanted that kind of relationship.

But was Judith right? Was I simply afraid of getting hurt? Sebastian had claimed to love me. He'd asked me to marry him. Then he'd cheated on me. Was I looking for reasons to break up with Keith because I was subconsciously convinced he was going to break up with me eventually?

Grrr. Why did relationships have to be so complicated?

"Zo, I have to go or I'm going to have some major messes to clean up if I don't get these dogs outside faster. Promise me you won't do anything until after the holidays. Give it that long, okay?"

It was like all the confidence I'd felt earlier about my decision was sucked out of my body through the phone. Of the two of us, Judith regularly made better decisions. What were the chances that I was right and she was wrong here? "Fine."

"Love you. Be safe."

"You too."

The call dropped.

I huffed out a breath of air. It's not like I was going to break up with Keith over the phone anyway, so it shouldn't matter that I'd promised to wait, right?

I needed Orion hugs. And I still needed to feed Teddy. Maybe he'd bark so loud that I wouldn't be able to hear myself think. For once, that would be a blessing.

I returned Tiffany's phone, swung by the cafeteria, and grabbed another packet of food, then headed back to the convention hall. Tiffany sat with her back to one of the walls, a book open in her lap and Orion flopped out on his side next to her. Darcy, Mason, and Graudin were gone. Simone sipped water from a bottle, in between pouring small amounts into her palm for Lucy to drink.

I shook my head and turned toward Teddy's crate.

The door wasn't latched. His crate was empty.

11

I spun back around. Where had he gone? The cafeteria wasn't that far down the hall. I would have heard barking if one of the others decided to take Teddy out for a bathroom break.

"Tiffany?"

She looked up at me.

I pointed at Teddy's crate. "Where did Victoria's dog go?"

She turned her gaze to follow where I was pointing. Her mouth hung open slightly. "I thought he was sleeping."

How could this have happened? Was he some sort of Houdini dog? "Did you hear any barking in the night?"

Tiffany shook her head. "And I'm not a heavy sleeper. His barking would have woken everyone up."

There was no doubt about that. More than one of us had likened his barking to a fire alarm or a siren. Ryan and

I probably would have heard him all the way down the hall.

But then how did he get loose? He barked when anyone went near him. He couldn't have been drugged or killed by the murderer. Teddy would have still barked when they got close, before they could silence him. Theoretically, maybe someone might have been able to throw a sedative and hit his crate so it would fall in? Simone *was* low on her anti-anxiety meds, but most dogs wouldn't eat naked pills.

And why would anyone bother? What purpose could the murderer possibly have for smuggling Teddy out in the night? It wasn't like they were afraid of Teddy identifying them by barking or growling at them. He did that with everyone.

I went over to the crate. The crate door hung open wide enough that Teddy could have easily left on his own.

Tiffany got up and joined me, Orion coming with her. "Could you have forgotten to secure his crate after you fed him last night?"

I ran last night back in my memory. I'd been trying to get away from him as quickly as possible so he'd stop barking and not choke on his food. "I thought I locked it, but it's possible."

Tiffany shook the crate. It wobbled. "The crate doesn't exactly look new. The hooks might not even fasten correctly. Or he might have found a way to wiggle out."

In my experience, cats found their way out of crates

more often than dogs did. Most people didn't realize how narrow a slot a petite cat could squeeze through.

I knelt on the ground for a better look. The bars of the crate weren't new, but they weren't bent anywhere, either. Certainly not enough to provide an escape route for Teddy. His blankets weren't even disturbed. If he'd dug at the crate and worried at the bars until something came loose, his blankets should have been mussed up at the very least. I must not have closed the door correctly. Now it was my responsibility to find him again.

I turned back to the room. Graudin had returned, but Mason and Darcy were still gone.

I waved at Graudin and Simone until they looked at me. "Victoria's dog got out in the night. Did you notice anything?"

"Good riddance." Graudin bent over and retied his boot lace. "Much longer with that dog and we'd all have had permanent hearing damage."

Simone shot him a dirty look, then turned toward me. "Sorry. I didn't see anything."

Leo stirred slightly, but he didn't wake up even with our calling back and forth across the room. The man clearly slept so soundly that he wouldn't have heard anything.

I'd have to hunt down Darcy and Mason and see if either of them knew anything.

I took Orion's leash back from Tiffany and headed in the direction of the nearest women's bathroom. That seemed like the most likely place to find Darcy.

I pushed the door open.

"You don't understand the position it put me in." Darcy's voice came from the side, as if she were talking to someone from inside one of the bathroom stalls.

A pause.

"That's not funny," she said.

Definitely on the phone. Which was good, because if she were talking to Mason in the ladies' room, that would have been weird.

I leaned against the door. I'd wait for her to finish rather than interrupting her.

"You're not listening." Darcy's voice rose slightly. "I'm not doing that again. We were—"

She cut off as if the person on the other end had talked over what she was trying to say.

"That's not true." A quiver had entered her voice. "I'm sorry you feel that way."

An uncomfortable tightness filled my body. This wasn't a normal conversation. This was an argument with someone she was close to. I shouldn't be overhearing this.

I backed up. The door to the stall Darcy had been in swung open, and her gaze met mine.

"I have to go." There was a hiss to Darcy's words. She bent her head down as if that would prevent me from listening in. "No, we just have to talk about this later, okay?"

She pulled the phone away from her ear and looked at it. A slightly stung expression flashed across her face.

Had the person she'd been talking to hung up on her? That was childish and rude.

Darcy faced me. Red splotched her cheeks and rimmed her eyes.

I stepped inside the restroom, bringing Orion with me, and let the door fall shut behind me. Leaving now would only make it worse. "I'm really sorry. I didn't mean to eavesdrop."

Her mouth opened a sliver, as if she'd been prepared to yell at me and hadn't expected a sincere apology.

She shook her head in a resigned way. "Were you looking for me, or did I just pick the wrong place to try to have a private conversation?"

I explained about Teddy.

She pulled a piece of paper towel from the dispenser and touched the edge beneath her eyes. "I didn't see anything during my shift watching Leo. And that dog's so loud I can't imagine anyone let him out while I was asleep, either."

I swallowed down a snort. Teddy had certainly managed to earn a reputation in the short time we'd been together. "If you spot him, give me a..." I touched a hand to the pocket where I normally shoved my cell phone. "I don't have my phone at the moment. Bring him to either Tiffany or Detective MacIntosh." I didn't want her putting him back into the crate only for him to escape again if he'd found a way. Once an animal knew how to get out of a confined space, there was no way you'd be able to keep them in. And they'd only get faster each time. "Could you let Mason know if you see him first?"

Darcy nodded into the mirror, not looking my way.

I turned for the door, Orion practically underfoot in the small space, blocking my path out the door. He turned his face up, his tongue lolling out, as if to say *You're not done yet.*

Judith should have been the one trapped here instead of me. Not that I would have wanted her to have to deal with dead bodies and missing dogs, but she had a much softer shoulder for people to cry on.

Unfortunately for Darcy, I was what she got.

I swiveled back around. "Are you going to be okay?"

Darcy met my gaze in the mirror. She blinked rapidly. "I'm not sure how to answer that, to be honest."

"If you need someone to talk to..."

Darcy gave a tiny smile. "I appreciate the offer."

Which was a nice way of saying *I'm absolutely not going to take you up on that.* I couldn't blame her. I wouldn't bare my soul to someone who was practically a stranger, either. It'd clearly been embarrassing enough for her to have me overhear whatever it was I'd overheard. Seemed like I wasn't the only one dealing with personal problems, and whatever Darcy was going through sounded worse than my dilemmas.

Darcy nodded at me in the mirror. "I'll look for Mason as soon as I'm done here and ask him about the dog."

I nudged Orion to his feet and herded him out the door. I wasn't about to sit around and wait for Mason to tell me the same thing everyone else had. Might as well get started looking for Teddy now.

I headed off in the opposite direction from where Victoria's body lay. Presumably, if Teddy had gone by Ryan and me in the night, either he would have barked at us or Orion would have tried to reach him. I'd slept with the loop of Orion's leash around my wrist. I would have known if he got up and attempted to follow Teddy somewhere. Which meant Teddy's most likely route was in the opposite direction.

I climbed up the opposite stairs from where Victoria fell, just like when I'd first found Teddy with his leash tangled around the radiator.

I ran over last night in my head again. I'd been a vet for years. I'd closed hundreds, if not thousands, of crates and cages. Surely I wouldn't have mislatched this one. But if I hadn't, that brought me back in a circle again to someone letting Teddy out of the cage. And that seemed impossible without everyone who'd been sleeping in the same room waking up when he barked.

We approached the radiator where I'd first found Teddy, and I stopped, even though this time he couldn't have been tangled up in the same spot. The first time, he'd been wearing his leash. This time he had only his collar.

I stared at the radiator. Something about it niggled at the back of my mind now that I was carefully looking at it alone without being focused on freeing a dog. How had Teddy managed to tangle himself up that first time? The leash hadn't been merely snagged on the radiator. It'd been almost looped around.

At the time, I was so happy to find him that I hadn't thought much about how he'd done it. Plus, I assumed Victoria's death was accidental. Who automatically thinks murder when it looks like someone has fallen down the stairs? Not me, at least. I hadn't been suspicious about how his leash was wrapped around the radiator at the time.

I'd had to work it free, though.

I put Orion into a stay, took off his leash, and replicated the snarled-up mess I'd found Teddy's leash in as well as I could.

"Teddy couldn't have done that himself," I said to Orion.

Orion cocked his head at me as if to say, *You're the expert. I don't have opposable thumbs.*

Someone had tied Teddy up. I was sure of it. For whatever reason, they hadn't wanted Teddy to be found right away. As unlikely as it seemed, Teddy must somehow hold the key to who killed Victoria. Enough that her murderer had stolen him from the crate in the night and either killed him, too, or hid him. Hopefully the latter. I had to think that if the murderer had chosen to tie Teddy up the first time rather than killing him as well, then whatever had stopped the killer the first time might stay his or her hand again. There was still a good chance Teddy was alive somewhere.

I needed to rewatch the surveillance video. The clue to why Teddy was such a threat might be on there. Could he have nipped Victoria's attacker and swallowed a piece of material that could identify the killer? I didn't remember him showing any aggression in the video, but I had been more focused on what was about to happen to Victoria than on anything else.

I snapped Orion's leash back on his collar, and we set off to the security office. I stopped in front of the door.

The closed and locked door.

Ryan had locked the door after we watched the video of Victoria's death, and when I caught Leo, he hadn't managed to unlock it yet.

I knelt down in front of the lock the way Ryan had done when he picked it. The knob itself didn't have a locking mechanism. The door locked using a deadbolt.

If I went to get Ryan, I might not get to rewatch the video. One of us would have to stay with Victoria's body. I needed to see the video as soon as possible. The niggling in the back of my brain told me I was missing something. I couldn't let the pieces slip away before I could fit them together.

Maybe I could pick the lock the way Ryan had. How hard could it be? Surely there were videos online to teach that sort of thing. Weren't you supposed to be able to do it with a hair pin? I always had those handy. I rested my hand on the knob and leaned in for a better look.

The knob twisted underneath my hand, and the door swung open. I toppled forward. My elbows slammed into the floor, and shards of pain flashed up my arms as if I'd hit both funny bones. Orion bounced after me, lunging in, trying to lick my face. My arms hurt so much I couldn't even block him. His tongue slurped all over the side of my face. Clearly he thought we were playing a new kind of game.

The only way to spare the rest of my face was to get off the floor, pain or no pain. I hoisted myself to my feet and dropped into the rolling chair closet to the monitors. The door was one of those weighted ones. It closed automatically behind me. Which was for the best. I'd dropped Orion's leash when I smashed my elbows.

I rubbed both elbows. The pain had eased from *I shoved my arm through a glass window pane* to a dull ache. How had the door gotten unlocked? Had Leo managed to get the right key the moment before I found him? I'd have to ask Ryan if he'd checked the door after we caught Leo.

Orion snuffled around the floor, sticking his nose into every corner, while I turned on the viewing monitor. The screen flared to life. The video wasn't paused where we'd left it. The screen glowed slightly, but it was blank.

Ryan had typed something into the keyboard to bring up the proper video. He'd had it written in his notebook, presumably told to him by whoever regularly ran the system. But he'd also looked in a binder when he'd wanted to know if there was a way to turn on sound for the recording.

I looked around. The black binder still lay open on the desk. The first page was a table of contents. I ran a finger down it until I found the part on playing back recorded footage.

Perfect.

I followed the instructions as written, but nothing happened. That was weird. Had I missed a step? I did it again. No change. The screen stayed blank and static.

I flipped back a few pages and read through anything that could apply, then followed the instructions to make sure everything was turned on correctly. No problems there. All the proper lights were lit. I tried one more time.

Nothing.

Uncomfortable flutters filled my stomach. The system was acting the way I'd expect if there was no recorded footage to play. That wasn't possible. Unless someone came in and erased the recording.

Ryan had stopped the system. He hadn't wanted to risk taping over Victoria's murder. If someone came in and erased what was already recorded, the system wouldn't be able to play anything for me.

I glanced back at the door. That would also explain why the door hadn't been locked. They'd unlocked it, but hadn't bothered to lock it again once they finished, maybe too worried about getting caught the way Leo was.

Tension tightened around my head, and I pressed my fingers gently into my temples. Maybe I was wrong. I wasn't an expert in this system. I probably should have gone to get Ryan in the first place.

I stood and picked up Orion's leash. That's what I'd do now. I'd get Ryan, and he'd come check for the recording. No doubt he'd be able to find it, and then he could queue it up for me to watch. Hopefully seeing it would let my brain resolve what'd been bothering me. Hopefully it'd still be soon enough that I didn't lose whatever break-through hovered an inch beyond my mental fingertips.

I turned the doorknob, but the door didn't budge. I glanced at the deadbolt. Locked.

Weird. I ran my entry into the room back through my mind. I'd only gone forward. I hadn't touched the door once I entered.

The door shouldn't be locked.

Cold followed by a wave of heat swept over the back of my neck, leaving tingles in its wake. I grabbed the deadbolt and wrenched upward.

The deadbolt refused to budge, as if someone had jammed something into the keyhole on the other side.

I wriggled it harder, pushing and pulling on the door. Nothing. I was locked in. Someone had locked me in.

12

My breaths came quick and ragged. I jammed my shoulder into the door while trying to force the deadbolt to turn. I tore the skin off my knuckle, but the deadbolt stayed stuck shut. I'd break my shoulder before I broke the door or the lock.

I sank to the floor and sucked on my knuckle until the pain eased slightly. I forced myself to take extra-long breaths. I was going to be fine. We were going to be fine. I wasn't five anymore, locked in a closet as punishment, not sure when Tonya would come back to let me out. Not sure how long it would be before she sobered up enough to remember she'd locked me in.

I intentionally looked around the room. Not nearly as small as that closet. I could move around in here without bumping into things. And I wasn't alone. I had Orion.

And I could just call Ryan. He'd come and let me out.

I reached into my pocket. My fingers met only fabric. My phone was plugged into the wall downstairs. I couldn't call Ryan or anyone else to rescue me.

Panic scrabbled up my throat and threatened to choke me. For a second, all I could see was the back of the closet door, the thin strip of light underneath during the day, and even that gone at night. The hunger gnawing in the pit of my stomach. The need to use the bathroom growing until I couldn't hold it anymore.

I called Orion over and stroked his soft ears and jowls. I wasn't that kid anymore. I wouldn't be her anymore, afraid of small spaces or anyplace I couldn't get out of. Paralyzed. I must have options. If I focused on my options, I could get through this.

I crawled to my feet and paced the length of the room. Surely someone would realize we'd gone missing and come looking for us. My gaze leapt back to the deadbolt.

Except no one would think to look here. Everyone believed this room was locked. Everyone other than the killer, who must also be the person who locked me in.

Ryan would realize I hadn't left as soon as he spotted my phone next to his and my car still in the parking lot. But he wouldn't immediately think he needed to run around looking for me.

And this was a large building. Once he did realize something was wrong, if he had to search everywhere, he might not find me until everyone else had left. That might have been the killer's whole reason for locking me in here. If the roads cleared before I was found, he or she would have a head start. They could disappear before the police had any way to prove they were the one who killed Victoria.

Plus, hiding me away the way they'd hidden Teddy meant Ryan wouldn't be continuing to investigate Victoria's death. He'd be distracted by trying to find me. He'd have to leave Victoria's body to find me. If the killer wanted to destroy or plant any evidence, that would give him or her the perfect window to do it.

I flopped back down in the chair. Orion dropped at my feet. I stroked his head again.

My throat closed up, threatening to choke me. Without water, we had two to three days. I might be able to survive a little longer than that, but Orion couldn't. And certainly not without major health consequences if he did survive.

His trusting eyes gazed up at me, his head tilted back, giving me perfect access to scratch his ears. I would get us out of here.

And whoever put my baby boy at risk was going to pay. Dearly.

I just had to figure out *how* to get us out of here first.

The desk didn't have a landline phone. The security officers must communicate by radios and cell phones.

I looked up at the ceiling. No air vents large enough for me to crawl out of. I swiveled the chair around. And nothing heavy enough that I could beat the door with until someone heard it.

I buried my face in my hands. They smelled like Orion.

Focus. Think. I had to find a way to let Ryan know we

were here and in trouble. I couldn't trust anyone else to find us. Not when I didn't know which of them had locked us in.

We were in the security office, so at least I could see where everyone was. That might give me some ideas.

I pulled the manual toward me again and turned on all the smaller monitors. The stairwells appeared, followed by the convention hall cameras, different views of the hallways, and the parking lot.

Darcy was nowhere to be seen on the monitors. Neither were Mason or Simone. The bathrooms didn't have cameras in them, for obvious reasons, so they could be in one of them.

Tiffany and Leo were in the convention hall. Leo still appeared to be sleeping. Tiffany must have gotten the morning shift for watching him. If they were together, that meant neither of them could have done this.

A bundled-up figure shoveled snow away from Graudin's truck. I could safely guess that was Graudin. Was he going to make another attempt at leaving even though snowplows hadn't come through yet? On one hand, that made him look guilty. On the other hand, there was no way he could have locked me in and gotten outside with enough time to make that much progress in clearing the snow. His truck was brushed bare, and he'd shoveled away the snow in a five-foot perimeter from the back half.

I continued checking the screens. Ryan still sat near Victoria's body. The camera angle showed his front. He was awake now, retying his tie.

A smile crossed my lips. He was going to make sure he had a straight tie and try to get rid of as many wrinkles as possible from his jacket, but there wasn't going to be anything he could do about his hair.

How did I let him know where we were and that we were in trouble? I flipped through the manual again. The security system was one-way. They also didn't have a speaker system hooked up to this room for announcements. That was done through the sound booth off of the convention hall so that people who rented the hall could use it for their own purposes.

So my only connection with the outside world was the cameras, and those seemed to be one way as far as I could tell. Had there been a light on them indicating whether they'd been on or not? If there had, I could switch them on and off in some sort of pattern. The only pattern I knew that wouldn't look completely random was the dot-dot-dot dash-dash-dash dot-dot-dot of an S.O.S. Ryan should know Morse code, shouldn't he? That seemed like something the academy might teach police officers. Besides, who didn't know S.O.S.? It was iconic.

My plan was better than nothing, though it depended on a light that I couldn't be sure existed and Ryan looking at one of the cameras long enough to recognize that the light wasn't flickering sporadically.

I checked the manual one more time so I was sure I was getting the sequence right. My dots were going to be a little long given that I had to press more than one button to turn the cameras on and off, but I'd lengthen my dashes accordingly.

Orion nuzzled his nose into my palm.

I stroked his head one more time. "I know, buddy. I'm going to try to get us out of here as soon as I can."

13

Could you bruise your fingertips? Mine certainly felt bruised from pushing these stupid buttons. I'd been at it for over an hour. Ryan still hadn't looked at the camera long enough to notice what I was doing. Assuming I *was* even doing anything. There might be no light there at all.

He had, however, made more than one phone call. To keep myself from focusing on where I was and that I couldn't get out, I imagined that he was getting details about Victoria's relationships from her mother. Digging deeper into the case so we might finally be able to figure out who'd killed Victoria and locked me in this room. And when that was done, laying the groundwork for us to find Harper so we could spend Christmas together. I made up entire conversations as I tapped.

Soft snores emanated from the floor behind me. At

least Orion had settled down after pacing the room and squeaking and scratching at the door for over half an hour.

I tapped the pattern into the stupid machine again.

"Come on. Look up. Look. Up. Up. Up. Up." Ryan was still talking into his phone. He'd started to wander down the hall. "Haven't you started to wonder where I am yet?"

I laid my head down on the desk, pillowed on my free arm. I'd try for another ten minutes, then I'd have to give up and take a break. I prayed in time to my button pressing. That made it a little more soothing.

Pounding rattled the door. I jerked upright, losing my spot in the sequence.

"Zoe?" Ryan's voice was loud and urgent.

I scrambled to my feet and pressed my hands flat against the door. "Someone locked me in!"

"Are you and Orion okay?"

"We're not hurt. Other than my hand from turning those cameras on and off. It took you forever to notice."

Ryan's laugh carried relief in it. "Was that supposed to be S.O.S.?"

I leaned my forehead against the door. "It was the only Morse code I knew."

"Let me see if I can get you out of there." His voice seemed to move down the door as he spoke.

"*If* doesn't exactly inspire confidence." My voice shook slightly. It made me feel pathetic that I couldn't control it, but this room was starting to feel smaller and smaller.

"I'm going to get you out." Ryan's voice had a distracted

note as if he were only half paying attention. "Just need to figure out how. Someone broke a key off in the lock."

I straightened slightly but kept my hands pressed against the door. That would explain why the deadbolt had refused to move. It couldn't. "They erased the recording of Victoria's death."

Ryan made a frustrated noise—either from the news I'd delivered, the state of the lock, or both. "I'm going to need a pair of pliers. A little bit of the key is still sticking out, but I can't get a grip on it."

I could almost hear him considering whether it could create problems to ask Leo if there was a tool kit in the building. Hunting for it himself without Leo's guidance could be a fruitless search, and it meant leaving us in here longer while also leaving Victoria's body unattended.

"It wasn't Leo or Tiffany. They were both in the convention hall when I turned on the cameras, looking for you. I don't think they could have gotten back there in time, and you can easily check to see if they were together the whole time."

"So I can ask Tiffany to watch Victoria's body while Leo helps me find some tools to get you free." His voice softened. "I'll try not to be long."

———

"MUCH LONGER?" I asked.

I sat on the floor next to the door. Orion alternated

between sniffing around the edges of the door again and squeaking at Ryan through the door.

I glanced at the clock. Forty-five minutes. Was the second hand even moving? It didn't look like it was moving anymore. If I closed my eyes for too long, I could smell musty clothing and see the bare, burnt-out lightbulb that used to hang in the closet Tonya would put me in.

Whatever therapist came up with the idea that you could deal with people's fears by exposing them to those fears had clearly never been truly afraid of anything themselves. Or maybe there was a difference between irrational fears, like when you were afraid of snakes even though a snake had never done anything to you, and trauma-based fears. Because being locked in that closet had hurt me, and I didn't want to be in this room anymore, stuck thinking about it over and over and—

The door swung inward.

I lunged to my feet and dodged past Ryan and Leo, who stepped back out of my way. I stood in the middle of the hallway and sucked in air. I didn't care what anyone said about the ventilation system. There was definitely more oxygen out here than there had been in that room.

Orion danced in a circle around Ryan. Ryan scrubbed him along his sides, then headed into the security office.

A shiver traced down my arms. I couldn't go back in there. Not right away. at least.

I forced my feet to move until I stood in the doorway. Leo hovered beside me, a toolbox at his feet, but Ryan didn't make him leave. Leo stifled a yawn. I glanced at him.

He looked droopy, like a stuffed animal who'd lost half its stuffing.

Ryan flipped open his notebook to use the same instructions as before. The screen stayed blank.

"Gone." He leaned back in the chair and rested his palms on the top of his head, in the posture of a man who didn't know what to do next. He rotated the chair to face me. "How did you get in here anyway?"

I could hear the unspoken question: *did you pick the lock?* Both because he'd told me not to and because, if I'd done it, whoever erased the video could have done it as well.

"The door was unlocked when I got here." He didn't need to know that I'd been considering picking the lock prior to finding the door unlocked. He probably suspected as much, but I might as well keep as much of my dignity as possible.

Ryan turned the security cameras off. "The lock was challenging to pick. Someone without training and the right tools couldn't have done it. So they likely had the actual key."

My gaze flickered to Leo. He was on one knee now, locking the toolbox back up. None of the others would have keys for the rooms in this building, but we knew Leo couldn't have locked me in. Maybe whoever erased the video found another set while looking for a better hiding spot for Teddy. "Leo, are there any sets of spare keys in the building?"

Leo shook his head. "Management says all keys have to

be kept on a person at all times. I wouldn't even turn my set over to Detective MacIntosh. It's my job if anything happened to them."

He reached a hand down and patted a spot on his belt. He froze, and his face went a pasty shade, as if someone had covered his skin with a concealer that was a shade too light.

Ryan straightened in the chair. "Are your keys missing?"

Leo nodded dumbly. He looked down at where his keys should have been. He felt around the rest of his belt, clearly hoping that they'd simply shifted. "I slept with them on. How could someone have gotten them off my belt?"

Ryan stood up and moved to the door. "Why don't you retrace your steps to the furnace room, make sure they didn't fall off?"

Fall off his belt? I'd seen those keys on Leo's belt. The key ring was the kind that had to be slid on before the wearer did up their belt. They couldn't have slipped off. "Check the men's room, too, just in case."

That was the only way I could think of that he could have lost them accidentally. We had been here long enough that Leo might have needed to undo his belt to take care of biological needs.

Leo scooped up the toolbox, not even waiting to acknowledge our suggestions. He strode down the hall, moving so quickly he was practically jogging. He didn't look entirely steady on his feet. He wasn't moving in a straight line.

Ryan came up beside me. We watched him go together.

I folded and unfolded the end of Orion's leash. "Do you think he could have slipped away in the night and erased the video, and then whoever locked me in here didn't want me snooping around for an entirely different reason?"

Ryan motioned for me to leave the security room. "Not unless someone fell asleep when they were supposed to be watching him. Which is possible. I'll talk to everyone. But it seems more logical that the real killer used that time alone to steal Leo's keys, sneak off, and erase the recording."

He closed the door behind us, but without the keys, he couldn't lock it again. Not that it mattered now. What we'd been trying to protect was gone.

"They managed to take Leo's keys. Do you think they also found a way to let Teddy out of his crate without being caught?"

Ryan matched my pace as we headed down the hall. "Releasing the dog would have been a risk. His barking could have woken everyone up. And I don't see how that would have helped them."

His words mirrored my thoughts from earlier. So Teddy had likely escaped on his own, unconnected to Leo's missing keys.

Getting those keys off of Leo's belt wouldn't have been easy. Leo's expression had been genuinely baffled about how anyone could have removed them.

I stuttered to a stop. That was it. "They're still missing."

Ryan kept moving for two more steps, then turned back. "What?"

I practically bounced on my toes. "Leo's keys."

Ryan raised his eyebrows. His expression said I was talking nonsense, but I wasn't.

I grabbed his arm and gave it a little shake. "The time they had to do all that was so short that they weren't able to return Leo's keys. They might still have them.

14

"Everyone step away from your belongings and form a line along the wall."

Ryan's voice had a *no arguments* ring of command. He seemed so calm—his shoulders straight, his arms relaxed at his sides, his gaze firm without being confrontational. He expected compliance. Were some people born feeling like others should listen to them? I certainly hadn't been. Every bit of space I took up, I had to earn. And fight to keep. If I wasn't vigilant, someone more worthwhile would show up and take it from me.

"What is this?" Graudin planted fisted hands on his hips, looking a bit like a farce of Superman. All he needed was a red towel as a cape. "Are you going to summarily execute us?"

"This isn't a communist country, Mr. Graudin." Ryan could have been a statue for the reaction he had to

Graudin's accusation otherwise. "I need to look for a piece of evidence. I don't want anyone trying to hide it. An innocent person won't have anything to hide. I'm going to assume everyone is fine with me checking the sleeping area?"

Technically, Ryan couldn't search their belongings without either probable cause, a person's permission, or a warrant, depending on the situation. The way he'd phrased it made it so that no one should object. Tacit permission.

I frowned slightly. Except the person who had the keys *should* object. They should be worried. I scanned the faces of each person in turn, but no one looked at all nervous. At least one person should have shown signs of stress if we were right. Had they disposed of the keys already? Maybe they'd tossed them in a trash can on their way back to the convention hall.

Ryan started with Tiffany's belongings even though we were sure she hadn't done it. As he cleared each person, he also asked if they'd fallen asleep while they were supposed to be watching Leo.

Tiffany was cleared, followed by Darcy and Graudin. The man might be a jerk, but it seemed less likely by the minute that he'd killed Victoria.

Ryan finished searching Mason's belongings. No keys.

"And did you fall asleep at any point while you were supposed to be watching Leo?"

Mason ran a hand down the front of his suit jacket, his

fingers bumping over the buttons. "I might have. I can't be sure. I'm not used to staying awake in the middle of the night."

Ryan looked like he wanted to swear, but he didn't. If Mason had fallen asleep, then Leo could have been lying about someone stealing the keys, though Leo had been with Tiffany when I was locked in the security office.

None of this seemed to fit together.

Ryan bent over Simone's bedding, lifted her jacket, and shook it. A set of keys on a heavy keyring dropped from the sleeve and clanked to the ground. One of the keys was missing its end. Not only were they Leo's keys, but they were definitely the set of keys belonging with the key that had been used to lock me in the security office.

Darcy's eyes went wide, and she looked toward Mason as if wanting someone to share her shock. Clearly, she hadn't had the same suspicions about Simone as I had. But I might not have suspected Simone at all if I hadn't put together the pieces about Victoria's potential sabotage.

Simone shot a glance at me and stepped back as if the keys might be radioactive. "Those aren't mine."

Her move made her seem even guiltier than finding the keys had. But she'd glanced at me first. It was such a similar action to the one that took place between Leo and Tiffany. Did Simone think I'd vouch for her innocence? Because we'd had a couple of chats?

Ryan pulled a plastic baggie from his pocket and scooped up the keys, probably more for show than to preserve evidence. "We know that. They're Leo's. Someone removed them from his belt last night and used them to erase the recording of Victoria's death."

"I didn't do that, either." Simone's mouth turned down at the corners, and she clutched Lucy to her. "I had no reason to."

"We're going to go have a talk about that." Ryan held an arm toward the door leading out into the hallway. "If you'll come with me, please."

I slid Orion's leash into Tiffany's hands and followed along with them. I'd come this far. Ryan surely wouldn't expect me not to take part in his conversation with Simone.

Ryan didn't take her all the way down to Victoria's body. He only brought her to where we'd laid out our beds last night.

Simone sucked her bottom lip in between her teeth. "I don't know how the keys got in my stuff. Maybe the person who took them dropped them. But I didn't have a reason to hurt Victoria."

Ryan brought his notebook out of his pocket and flipped through it. "Do you know who destroyed your dog biscuits yesterday?"

Simone tucked Lucy more securely in the crook of her arm and slowly shook her head. "I didn't see who—wait... you think it was Victoria, and I killed her over them? They were dog biscuits. It's not like she burned my house down with Lucy inside or anything."

She still looked hungover, with red rimming her eyes

and her face drawn, but her words were clear. The pills had worn off enough that she was able to focus and communicate clearly, unlike yesterday.

I frowned. She hadn't seemed disconnected this morning, but Leo had. He'd had trouble waking up, and he'd still been lethargic when he and Ryan freed me from the security office. Unsteady on his feet.

"How much did the loss set you back?" Ryan asked.

"Not enough to kill someone over." Her tone was equal amounts exasperated and confused, like she couldn't comprehend someone committing murder over something like that. "Maybe enough to sue her if I'd had proof. But I didn't see who did it. The vendor with the booth next to mine said the hot chocolate jug wasn't his. He thought the organizers set it up for people to have for free. The sign on it even said *Free Hot Chocolate*."

She looked directly at me. "I wasn't even going to continue the business. I told you that. I need something low stress. Baking that many biscuits and then hawking them like I'm some sort of street performer is the opposite of that."

She *had* told me that earlier, when she would have had no reason to lie to me. And we could confirm her story with the vendor whose booth was next to hers. If Simone had seen Victoria tip the hot chocolate over, she wouldn't have tried to get the other vendor to take responsibility. If the other vendor had seen Victoria do it, he'd tell us. More than that, Simone would have been able to take Victoria to small claims court for damage to her property. Or she could have told the police, and they could have traced whether Victoria bought the hot chocolate jug and the hot chocolate to fill it with.

But if I was right about Leo being drugged with Simone's pills, didn't that suggest she'd done it to steal his keys and erase the video? This wasn't adding up.

I made a timeout signal to Ryan behind Simone's back. A muscle at the corner of his eye twitched, and I could have sworn he would have rolled his eyes at me if he hadn't been in professional mode.

"Stay here, where I can see you," Ryan said to Simone.

He followed me. I cast one final glance at Simone. She had her face pressed into Lucy, who was licking her cheek with her teeny, tiny tongue. No dog tongue should be that adorable.

We stopped, and Ryan raised both his eyebrows. "Yes?"

Maybe if we talked this through, something would click. "Was Leo unusually groggy when you went to get him this morning?"

Ryan's eyebrows came down between his eyes. "He couldn't seem to focus for the first couple of minutes. I kept having to repeat myself. He apologized. Said he must not have slept well."

I shook my head. "I think someone drugged him with Simone's pills to make him less likely to wake up while they stole his keys." An image of Simone staring in confusion at her nearly empty pill bottle flashed across my mind. "But I don't think it was Simone. She was confused this morning when she had fewer pills left than she expected."

I recapped the conversation I'd had with her that morning.

Ryan nodded slowly. "Motive would be shaky at best if we're looking at Simone as a suspect. It might be out of my hands as soon as the roads open, though. We have nothing to suggest anyone else had a reason to want Victoria dead."

No one but Leo, and his motive had the same gaps in its foundation as Simone's.

"I'd plant the keys on someone else. If I were the killer. I wouldn't keep them." I closed my eyes to block out distractions. What we needed was a way to tie the keys back to whoever had stolen them. "What about finger-prints? On the keys. Only Leo's should be there."

Ryan pulled the baggie with the keys out of his pocket. "People watch crime shows. Most of them think about wiping prints away now."

I tapped a fingernail against my lips. "In a normal situation. But we're talking about late at night. It's like when you might forget to lock the door if your dog has to go out in the middle of the night. And they might have been counting on Simone touching them before you found them and smudging any prints they left."

Ryan turned the baggie over in his hands, end to end. "Clean keys would be suspicious, but it won't clear Simone. It would only mean she didn't have time to toss them after cleaning them."

"We could get lucky and find a print." I pressed my

hands into my thighs to keep from taking the keys from Ryan's hands out of sheer excitement. "Can you pull prints from the keys? I'm sure Simone and Leo will let you take their prints. Find one that doesn't match, and you'd have a reason to ask everyone else to supply prints."

15

"I don't carry a fingerprint kit with me." Ryan's gaze was slightly unfocused, as if he were making a list in his mind. "But I could do it with a few simple supplies. I'd need approval, though. I'm out of my jurisdiction."

The urge to hug him flooded through me. Sometimes my ideas went too far, like when I'd tried to convince him to teach me to pick locks. I really shouldn't be given the ability to break into places I wasn't supposed to be. That'd be too great a temptation.

But he always listened. He always went in believing what I said had value.

"What do you need? Maybe I can find it while you call the local police chief."

Ryan rattled off a list—clear tape, a soft brush, powder of some sort, and paper—then went to make the call. I had the tape and paper. The powder and brush would be more difficult. I rarely wore makeup, and I certainly didn't carry any around with me. We couldn't exactly run out to the store. If running to the store was that easy, the crime-scene techs could have gotten here already.

Back down the hall, Simone had settled down on the floor, her lap making a nest for Lucy. Simone's makeup looked almost perfect. She definitely had mascara and lipstick in her bag, because no one's lips were that shade of crimson naturally. And she'd been all smeary yesterday from crying. There was a chance.

I headed back down the hall and sat beside her, like an equal. No leaning over her like I was demanding something. "We think we've found a way to clear you."

Hope, then skepticism, flew across Simone's expression. "Is this a trick?"

Her voice was soft. Scared to believe. Like an owner who'd been convinced their pet was going to die, only to be told we'd saved them.

It caught me around the throat and choked me. This wasn't just a puzzle to solve. It wasn't just a way to distract myself from what was going on with Harper.

For Simone, for Leo, for all of them, this was their life if I got it in my head to prove they were the murderer. I'd been them not that long ago. It certainly hadn't taken me long to forget what it felt like.

I tried to run my fingers through my hair to smooth it out, but my wavy curls were too tangled. My fingers snagged and tugged. I pulled them back out. "I'm sorry you've had to go through this. Detective MacIntosh isn't the kind of detective who's willing to accuse random people of murder to make some quota. He really wants to figure out who killed Victoria. So do I."

Simone's eyes filled with tears. "This has already been such a hard year. Yesterday, all I wanted to do was go home. I didn't care enough about those biscuits to hurt anyone over them. And if I'd wanted to keep running my business, I could. I handed out all my business cards. People seemed more interested because they couldn't buy my products right away, like they thought I was already sold out rather than having nothing to begin with." She clamped her lips shut. "Sorry. Rambling."

Lucy planted her thumb-sized paws on Simone's chest and flicked her tongue out, catching a tear.

Simone laughed, which made Lucy lick harder. "She helps." She lured Lucy away from her face using the dinosaur from earlier. "I'd like a way to show I didn't kill anyone."

The way she cringed when she said *kill* convinced me more than anything that she hadn't. "Then I'd like to borrow your makeup if you have some powder and a brush."

Simone's lips quirked up to the side. "We're not exactly the same shade."

No arguing with that. Her skin was a beautiful tan, like she was sun-kissed even in the dead of a Michigan winter. I was more a pinky-yellow color. "Detective MacIntosh wants to pull prints from the keys."

Simone nodded along as I spoke. "Mine won't be on there. It'll show I didn't touch them."

"Exactly."

She confidently reached into her bag and pulled out a makeup case. She handed it all to me. "I have a couple mascaras in there, too. That might work if he needs to fingerprint people. They use black stuff on TV."

I hadn't thought about how Ryan would fingerprint people after he'd pulled the prints off the keys. He'd need some way to take prints to compare them to.

I tucked the makeup case under my arm. "Thank you."

Simone wiggled the dinosaur for Lucy, who pounced on it, not unlike a cat. "Do you think I need to stay here, or can I go back to the convention hall?"

Good question. I didn't want to screw up whatever plan Ryan might be putting in place. We wanted the real killer —assuming Simone was telling the truth—to think we weren't looking for them anymore. That must be why they planted the keys in her belongings. "Stay here for now."

Ryan approached from down the hall. I got up to meet him.

He put his cell phone back in his pocket and gave a brisk nod. "It's a go."

———

RYAN LAID the keys out on a table in the cafeteria. I'd still need to find Teddy before we left. Since Ryan didn't think his escape was connected to Victoria's murder, though, the fingerprints took priority.

Ryan and I both put on gloves, and I held Ryan's

phone, recording everything so there would be a record if necessary. He gently tapped Simone's makeup brush into her powder and swirled it over each of the keys in turn. As anything resembling a fingerprint turned up, he used a clear piece of tape to remove the fingerprint and place it on a sheet of white paper. He made notes next to each fingerprint about which key they'd come from and even which side.

I would have hated this part of his job. Though, presumably, Ryan didn't actually do this regularly. Collecting fingerprints would fall to the crime-scene techs.

Ryan pulled the final fingerprint, wrote his notes, and leaned over the sheet. I moved in next to him.

He scowled. "I forgot how small these are when they're not blown up digitally."

Oh, I could fix that. I darted over to where I'd left my purse and fished around inside. "Somewhere in here I have...there it is." I pulled out a magnifying glass.

Ryan gave me a look that I would have called smitten had he been looking at anyone else. "And why do you carry one of those around with you?"

I handed it to him. "In case I have to remove a splinter from a paw."

"I should have guessed." His voice sounded amused.

He drew the paper with Simone's fingerprints over next to the keys. I perched on one of the cafeteria chairs.

He went print by print, back and forth between them.

He straightened. "No match. Not even a partial one.

Simone was telling the truth about not touching these keys. Unless she wore gloves."

Which was possible. "Would you have as many clear prints if she did?"

"Not likely. We'd probably have more smudged prints than we do."

"What do we do next?"

Ryan leaned slightly against the table. "You ask Darcy, Mason, and William to join us."

William? Oh, right. Graudin. "All together?"

"We can't risk picking the wrong one first. We don't know what the killer will do if we make him or her nervous enough."

16

Graudin raised his eyebrows at the mascara bottle. "This is the stupidest thing I've ever seen. Are you sure you're a real police detective?"

Ryan didn't say anything, refusing to rise to Graudin's baiting the way I undoubtedly would have.

Graudin sighed and held out his hands. "Fine. Let's get this farce of police work over with. I'll be filing a complaint with your superior as soon as we get out of this place."

Ryan carefully collected Graudin's prints using a doctored cleaning sponge provided by Leo and moistened with Simone's mascara.

Darcy and Mason had staked out a spot a few tables away. Mason sat one chair away from Darcy, his left ankle resting on his right knee. He looked like he was the one in charge here, overseeing what was going on rather than being one of the people about to be fingerprinted. Darcy looked a bit like she was going to be sick, swallowing hard, her expression pinched.

Watching her, my stomach didn't feel that great, either. Was it going to be Darcy at the end of all this?

Ryan finished taking Graudin's fingerprints. Since we weren't at a police station using official means, he also had Graudin sign the bottom of the paper where Ryan had applied his fingerprints. He'd already labeled the sheets with each person's name.

Graudin held up his blackened hands. "Can I go wash this off now?"

Ryan pointed to an empty seat. "Not until I've checked them all."

Maybe I should have told Ryan before he started that Simone had waterproof mascara. The non-waterproof mascara that had run on her yesterday had been applied at home and hadn't been dropped into her bag because it was a nearly empty tube. She also hadn't brought any makeup remover with her. Graudin's—and everyone else's—fingers were going to be black for a while.

Darcy took her turn, followed by Mason. Ryan had to move quickly. The mascara wouldn't stay wet as long as regular ink would.

As Ryan finished taking each set of prints, I moved it to the side so they wouldn't smudge.

A silence that reminded me of an awkward first date fell over the room as Ryan examined the fingerprints.

He raised his head and pushed the first sheet to the side. "Mr. Graudin, you're free to go."

I glanced at Darcy and Mason. Neither of them looked surprised. Darcy was now sitting on her hands as if they were cold. She'd tucked her long skirt tight in around her legs as well. Thanks to her knee-high boots, she'd managed to somehow cover all her skin except her face.

Graudin shoved to his feet and marched out of the room, his expression smug.

Ryan bent his head over the next sheet. He moved the magnifying glass back and forth. He straightened.

The tension around his eyes and mouth said it all. He'd found a match.

"You can go Mrs. McGee. Mr. Randall, you'll need to stay here with us."

Darcy lowered her face into her hands. In relief? Though wouldn't she have wanted to get away from here as quickly as possible if that were the case?

Mason's posture didn't change. "I think you'll want her to stay."

Ryan set down the magnifying glass. "It's not her prints on the key to the security office."

"No," Mason leaned back, opening himself up even more, "but she *is* the reason mine are."

17

D arcy burst into tears.

I looked between her and Mason. What in the world was going on here?

Darcy lifted her head and opened her mouth as if to speak, but a sob slipped out instead. She covered her face back up. It reminded me of the scene in the awful 2005 *Pride and Prejudice* remake where the actress playing Elizabeth Bennett kept coming into the room, losing control of her emotions, and fleeing the room again.

If Darcy had killed Victoria, at least she felt guilty about it. That had to mean something. Perhaps she'd simply confess to what she'd done now. Ryan could record her confession or have her write it out and sign it, and that'd be all that was needed. Simone and Leo wouldn't face further interrogations after we got out of here.

Darcy's weeping deepened and dug into my heart. Murderer or not, she looked so lost and alone. I slid into the seat next to her, on the opposite side from where Mason sat, and placed a hand gently on her back. Her crying increased for a moment, then tapered off.

She finally raised her face. Her skin was splotchy from crying. "It's not what you think."

Why did people always say that? Like it was supposed to convince the person listening that they were innocent without them having to share any details?

"I need to remind you of your rights," Ryan said softly, "before you go any further."

He rattled off the Miranda warning.

Darcy pulled a tissue from her pocket and wiped her face. Her motions were slow. "Maybe I would be better off waiting until I can speak to a lawyer."

I slumped back in my seat. If she decided not to say anything, Ryan couldn't force her to talk. Off to the side of us, Ryan was quietly repeating the same words to Mason.

Mason's expression suggested that he was barely listening. He wasn't taking this seriously at all, even though he was the one we could prove had taken Leo's keys. If Darcy wouldn't talk, maybe Mason would.

She must have told him something if he'd been willing to steal the keys for her. Or she'd seduced him into helping her. She wore a wedding ring, but that didn't mean she wouldn't have violated her wedding vows if she thought it would help her avoid being convicted of murder.

A tiny, heavy ball formed in my chest. What was I doing? I didn't know if Darcy would be willing to do that kind of thing. I didn't know anything for sure unless one of them talked.

I shifted position to face Ryan. "Isn't tampering with evidence a felony in Michigan?"

The corner of his lip twitched as if he wanted to smile at me, then all expression vanished from his face again. "A sentence of ten years in a murder case." He directed a firm gaze at Mason. "That applies to you as well."

Mason stiffened slightly. He didn't change posture so much as all his lines seemed to tighten, as if he'd clenched his muscles. "You can't prove that I knew what she was going to do."

I pursed my lips. "So she asked you to get her the keys for the security office, and you did it without wondering what she needed them for?"

Ryan raised his eyebrows at me. I clamped my mouth shut. Right, not the police detective here. It was one thing for me to help. It was another for me to accidentally take over. I wouldn't want Ryan barging into my clinic and acting like he was the veterinarian. That line shouldn't have been so hard to walk. I didn't *actually* think I knew everything. Ryan had all the training.

"As long as you didn't participate in the murder of Victoria Swanson, I'll advocate for leniency on tampering with the evidence if you explain to me what you did and why." Ryan's voice sounded so reasonable. Like he actually wanted to help them, but they needed to work with him.

Darcy sniffled. She glanced at Mason, and he nodded. "It's so embarrassing. I only told Mason after I learned there were cameras. I thought he'd understand because of what happened with his sister and her ex-husband." Red spread over Darcy's cheeks like some sort of infectious rash. "I work with vulnerable people. All it takes to lose my job is a hint of anything sexual."

She dropped her voice on the last word. I barely caught it.

Sexual—but not with Mason. She'd humbled herself to tell Mason about it because she needed his help to erase the recording.

Ryan cast me a look that clearly said *Please stay quiet and let her talk*. My desire to ask questions must have been plastered all over my face.

Darcy opened her mouth, closed it, and swallowed hard. "My husband..." She chewed on her bottom lip. "He's been pressuring me to do things I don't want to do. He said he'd need to cheat to get his needs met if I didn't."

This didn't sound like it had anything to do with Victoria at all, though Victoria had by all accounts been a serial cheater herself. Perhaps her husband cheated with Victoria.

"He came here with me today, and Victoria was flirting with him all morning."

It was like she'd read my mind.

Darcy swallowed again, as if whatever was blocking her throat was getting bigger and bigger with every word she spoke. "He made sure to tell me there were lots of women who wouldn't hesitate to do the things he was looking for. That other women found it exciting. Why couldn't I at least try it?" Her words dropped in volume until she was whispering. "I was scared he'd turn to Victoria if I didn't finally agree, so I was intimate with him in a public place. In the hallway."

I clenched my teeth. The way she said *intimate* let me know exactly what she meant. How dare he do that to her? I couldn't even begin to sort through all the ways in which what he did was wrong, not the least of which was that she could lose a job that was clearly important to her if they'd been caught.

But now it made sense. That was what she'd wanted erased from the recording. The irony was, she and her husband might not even have been caught on the recordings. With the number of blind spots in the building, there was a good chance she'd done all this for nothing.

"I called him this morning. I told him I wouldn't do that again, and he—" She cut off suddenly. She looked straight at Ryan for the first time since she'd started telling her story. "You don't need to know exactly what he said to me after do you?"

Ryan shook his head. "No ma'am. That's alright."

The compassion in his tone made me want to hug him on Darcy's behalf.

She bobbed her head. "After we finished yesterday, he took off. We'd driven separately because he had to go into work, and I wanted to stay for all the events. I didn't even enjoy them. I felt so dirty and used." She wiped at her nose with the tissue. "Anyway, then I learned about the cameras. I had to erase the recording. My job..."

Tears trickled down her cheeks. She cast a pleading look at Mason.

He lowered both feet to the ground. "She came to me because my sister's husband cheated. She thought I'd have compassion on her rather than judging, and I might help her fix it. I don't remember which of us came up with the idea to erase the video, but it was the only option."

Darcy glanced in his direction and blinked rapidly. Something he said surprised her. The only statement it could be was that he didn't remember who'd suggested erasing the video.

Mason leaned forward slightly. "I lifted the keys off Leo and gave them to Darcy. That's why my fingerprints were on them."

Mason was definitely leaving things out. The hole in that story itched at my mind. Which one of them stole Simone's medication and drugged Leo so that he'd sleep more soundly? I'd handled the pill bottle too much for us to get any decent prints off of it.

The memory of Mason performing sleight-of-hand tricks flashed across my mind. Stealing things and sliding drugs into someone's food or drink required the same dexterity and misdirection skills as so-called magic tricks did. Of course Mason would have been the one who'd have been able to get Leo's keys off his belt. His skills might even have subconsciously impacted Darcy's decision to ask him for help. Both she and Simone were watching his magic tricks yesterday.

But Mason likely wouldn't admit to drugging Leo if

pressed. It was one thing to admit to stealing keys. It was another thing entirely to dope someone up. For all he knew, Leo could have been allergic or had a bad reaction to the medication and died.

"Which one of you erased the video?" Ryan asked.

Darcy's lips parted.

Mason held up a hand toward her, then swung his gaze to Ryan. "I don't think we should say any more until we have a deal in writing. Neither of us wants to serve jail time for this."

An uncomfortable twitchy feeling built at the base of my throat. "Which one of you locked me in the security office?"

A frown line formed between Darcy's eyebrows—the kind that said *What are you talking about?*

Mason's lips thinned, and he shook his head. "After we erased the video, I wasn't sure I could get the keys back on Leo's belt without waking him up. We erased everything without watching it to try to be quick, but we were racing against time. We thought the safest thing would be to drop them in someone else's belongings. We don't know what happened to them after that."

He was sticking closely to *we* to make sure he didn't give anything away about who'd actually done it. Maybe they had done it together, but it seemed unlikely. One of them would have had to stay in the convention hall to act like they were guarding Leo. My guess was that Darcy had stayed. Even after Ryan checked for her prints, we wouldn't be able to confirm it unless one of them confessed, though.

Darcy could have been smart enough to wear gloves when touching the keys. Mason probably couldn't have clandestinely gotten them off of Leo's belt with his sense of touch dulled by gloves, hence why his prints were there.

No one else's prints had been on the keys except Leo's. Technically someone else could have worn gloves as well, but it seemed far-fetched to believe that Mason or Darcy hadn't been the one to lock me in the security office. They'd both been in the convention hall when Tiffany handed me her phone so I could talk to Judith. Either of them could have known or guessed that I didn't have my own phone. One of them must have done it.

I glanced at Ryan, but his expression was closed off as usual. He motioned for me to follow him.

"You two," he nodded toward Darcy and Mason, "stay here."

18

The cafeteria door swung shut behind us, and we did our routine of moving far enough down the hall to avoid eavesdropping while staying close enough to make sure they didn't sneak out. We didn't even have to talk about it anymore.

With us watching the cafeteria door, Mason and Darcy weren't going anywhere. The only other ways out of the room were the fire door at the back of the cafeteria, which would set off an alarm, and the freight door into the kitchen, which was chained shut.

I planted my hands on my hips. "You don't actually believe that someone else locked me in the security office, do you?"

Ryan swiped a hand through his hair, as if the lack of gel loosened more than just his curls. "I don't think they locked you in together. Darcy probably did it to delay us from finding out that the recording was erased."

I worried my bottom lip between my teeth. That would make sense. If she could have prevented me from telling anyone about the erased video until she was already gone, that would have worked in her favor. Sort of.

Though Mason's prints would have still been on the keys, and that would have eventually led back to her once he was questioned. Wiping the key clean would have been suspicious, the way Ryan and I had reasoned before. But wouldn't that have been safer than leaving his prints? He'd planted the keys on Simone. If he'd wiped the keys down, we would have known they were planted, but we wouldn't have known he was the one who planted them.

"Does it feel too convenient to you that Mason left his prints on the key?"

Ryan rubbed the side of his hand across his forehead as if that would clear up his thoughts. "People make mistakes when committing crimes. It's almost a guarantee. All that adrenaline fogs up their brains. And Darcy's the one with the motive to kill Victoria."

"What? Darcy explained why she erased the recording. It had nothing to do with wanting to get rid of the video of Victoria's fall."

The corners of Ryan's mouth drooped. "She admitted that Victoria was flirting with her husband. She was afraid he was going to cheat on her. That's motive. She could have lied to Mason about why she needed to delete the video."

My shoulders slumped. He was right, of course. But the shame in her voice when she'd confessed why she'd been desperate to erase the video kept rattling around in my head. Could she have faked that? She'd seemed ready to choke on her tongue when trying to spit it out.

I tapped the jacket pocket where he kept his phone. "You need to check her story with her husband. I don't think she killed Victoria. Not if she did what she said she did with her husband."

Ryan slid his hand into his pocket but didn't immediately take his phone out. "Explain."

Explain. Like I had it all worked out already. It was more like I was humming bits of a song that I couldn't remember the name of. "She was ashamed of what she did. And it was a much lesser offense than killing someone." I held up one finger, followed by a second. "And she wouldn't have needed to kill Victoria. She gave in to her husband."

"But then she wished she hadn't. She could have blamed Victoria for making her give in. She may have misdirected her anger at her husband and at herself." Ryan pulled out his phone. "I would have confirmed her story anyway, but it might not matter. She looks guilty."

"Because that's all that matters." Fire flamed up in my chest. "Not whether she's actually innocent."

He raised his hands up like I made him so angry he wanted to pull on his hair. He looked like he wanted to tell me not to be an idiot. Instead, he swallowed whatever he'd been about to say and sucked in a breath. "You can't make them all innocent. One of them has to be guilty."

I ran my hands over my face. It was going to have to be

one of the people here. Ryan was right. I couldn't make them all innocent by wishing it so. Even nasty Graudin had children at home. If it were him, all I'd be able to think about was what would happen to those kids. Having a parent in prison carried a stigma you couldn't escape. Even now, people who learned about Tonya sometimes assumed I would be a criminal, too. No child deserved to carry that load around with them.

"I just feel bad for her."

"This is part of police work." Ryan's voice was gentle. "Sometimes you wish you could look the other way because the person has gone through enough. But you can't."

I nodded. If the evidence pointed to Darcy, she'd stand trial. It wasn't up to me to decide whether she was guilty or innocent. I was here to help Ryan as much as I could until other officers could arrive. If we hadn't been trapped here, I wouldn't have even been involved in the investigation.

I sighed. As much as the puzzle behind murder investigations captured me the way a difficult diagnosis for one of my patients did, I would have made a terrible police officer. "Mason was just so ridiculously cocky."

Ryan laughed. "Too bad we ended up stranded here with so many other people. Imagine if it'd been just the two of us."

I rolled my eyes. "If I'm imagining that, then I'm adding warm weather and better food. And comfortable accommodations. Then it'd be perfect."

Heat seared into my cheeks. That sounded a bit too

much like I was suggesting my ideal weekend would be one spent alone with him.

He cleared his throat.

Why did I have to go and make it awkward? I did *not* want to accidentally make things weird between us.

"They're opening the roads." Graudin's voice carried down the hall. "A snow plow went by. Just watched it."

Darcy and Mason poked their heads out of the cafeteria.

I stepped back, putting extra space between Ryan and me. "I need to find Teddy. We can't abandon him here."

Ryan nodded. "You'll have to go by yourself." He hooked his thumb toward Darcy and Mason. "I need to clarify a few things before they try to leave."

This case would be more difficult to solve once everyone scattered and had time to consult with lawyers if they wanted to, but it seemed like we'd done everything we could. Once I found Teddy, I'd collect Orion and the three of us would head home. The police and district attorney would decide who, if anyone, to charge with Victoria's murder.

19

Teddy wasn't on the upper level. I pushed on every door to see if any were unlocked and checked in every space even remotely large enough for a Yorkie. The main floor was equally a bust. I already knew he wasn't in the convention hall or the cafeteria. I checked all the bathrooms—even the men's rooms after knocking and calling inside—on the off chance that he'd managed to push the heavy doors open.

That left only the basement or outside. Presumably someone would have mentioned it had he escaped outdoors when they were going in or out. Though I couldn't be sure about Graudin. The man seemed callous toward Teddy, considering he owned a pet store.

I located the basement door. It was marked *Employees Only*. It wasn't a swing door. It had one of the lever handles that only seemed to be found in public buildings. Teddy wouldn't have been able to reach it, let alone pull it down, while pushing on the door to open it.

If he were in the basement, someone had put him there. Which meant someone had taken him from his crate without being heard, as impossible as that seemed.

I pushed open the door and went down the industrial-style metal stairs, keeping my hands on the metal railings on both sides. It was like descending into a different world. The air was warmer and humid. A giant furnace whirred in the corner. Tanks large enough that I could have drowned in them probably provided the hot and cold water for the building. Pipes of all sizes ran across the ceiling, and jugs of chemical cleaners lined metal shelves on the wall. The place smelled faintly of dust and bleach.

Overall, the room was about the size of the cafeteria, minus the kitchen, but there were a lot of places a small dog could hide. But if someone had brought him down here, would he be hiding, or would they have tied him up somewhere?

"Teddy?" My voice bounced back at me as if the metal was reflecting it.

No response. Not that I should have been expecting one. Teddy wasn't actually his name. It's not like he would try to come when I called. And he'd been quiet in the convention hall while crated, despite people talking all around him.

A shiver ran over my body. The dim lighting and wheezed groans from all the pipes were spooky. At least I'd gotten my phone back from Ryan. If someone tried to lock me in here, I could call him for a rescue.

I moved clockwise around the room. The hot-water tanks and furnace gave off enough heat that sweat popped out on my upper lip. I gave them a wide berth. No one would have tried to hide Teddy behind them. He'd have suffered heat stroke.

I approached the first cold-water tank. A high-pitched bark yapped out above the background noises of the room.

I darted forward. Someone had attached a leash to Teddy's collar and tied him behind the water tank. He pulled the leash taunt, straining toward me, barking the whole time. A puddle a few feet away suggested he hadn't been able to hold his bladder this long.

Poor boy. I unknotted his leash. No way this could be mistaken for a tangle. Whoever brought him down here tied multiple knots. They probably hadn't wanted to risk him getting loose and scratching at the door. That could have led to his discovery.

I pulled out my phone and dialed Ryan. Teddy's barking was so loud I couldn't even hear if it was ringing. I dropped the leash and let him roam free. He wouldn't be able to get out of the basement without me, so he should be safe.

Teddy's barking stopped. I glanced back over my shoulder. He sniffed around like he was following a trail.

Ryan answered before the call was about to go to voicemail.

I didn't even wait for a hello. "I found him. He didn't

get out of the crate on his own. Someone tied him up down in the utility room in the basement. I'm sure whoever did it also killed Victoria."

Silence stretched on Ryan's end. "I'm trying to think of an argument against that conclusion, but I can't. I also can't think of a good reason why they'd need to steal the dog."

Neither could I. "Did the video show Teddy biting the attacker? Anything like that?"

"Not that I remember," Ryan said. "Come on up. We can talk about it more later. Everyone's getting ready to leave."

"You need to talk to them about Teddy before they do. Before they have a chance to practice lying about it. Wait, no! We should see who's surprised to see him. Whoever tied him down here probably expected him not to be found."

"I'll gather everyone in the cafeteria."

"Without telling them the real reason."

"Zoe." His tone carried a warning note.

Right. I didn't need to micromanage him. He was smart. He was well-trained. He knew what he was doing. "Sorry. Got carried away."

"I'll see you in a few minutes." The undertone of laughter was back in his voice.

I really loved that about him.

I turned around. "Come on, Teddy."

Motion on the stairs. My gaze snapped to it. Mason stood on the bottom step, blocking my path out.

20

I gasped, choked slightly, and was swallowed by a coughing fit.

Mason held up his hands in a placating gesture. "I didn't mean to surprise you. The roads are open. We're all sorting out belongings and packing up."

A cord of tension wrapped around my throat. The basement wasn't the obvious place to look for me, if that'd been his intent. He couldn't possibly have had time to search the rest of the building. And even if he had, maybe I was outside at my car.

"Thanks. I can't wait to get out of here." I tried to keep my voice level and casual. It wavered slightly anyway. "How did you know to find me here?"

Mason stepped off the stairs as if to allow me the chance to go first. "I didn't. I heard someone talking. I figured someone stepped down here for a private conversation and might not have heard the good news."

My throat released, and my breathing eased. That made sense. Darcy had tried to find a place for a private conversation earlier only to have me intrude by accident. Not everyone was okay with having their phone calls overheard.

And checking to make sure I'd heard the news instead of being left behind was thoughtful. I would have likely done the same thing.

Teddy came out from behind a pipe near the stairwell, dragging his leash behind him. I braced for the cacophony of barking to resume.

He stopped at Mason's feet, looked up at him, wagged his tail, and moved on.

My throat closed so tightly I wasn't sure how I was still able to breath. Teddy hadn't barked at him. He'd greeted him calmly and almost affectionately.

Just like he'd done with the person in the video who'd pushed Victoria down the stairs. Ryan and I had commented on how calm Teddy had seemed. He hadn't felt threatened by the person who'd pushed Victoria.

Why hadn't I thought of that sooner? That must be why Mason wanted the video erased and why he hadn't wanted to go anywhere near Teddy. He'd known it would be obvious that he was the person in the video. Teddy barked at everyone else.

Mason had used Darcy and her indiscretion as an excuse to get rid of the evidence. A good enough excuse that I'd believed him.

The only reason Teddy wouldn't bark at Mason was if he knew him well. Which meant Mason and Victoria weren't strangers the way he claimed. Mason and Victoria were the only two who were regularly on the dog show circuit—him showing his dogs and her selling her product. He could have met Victoria and Teddy dozens of times over the years.

Maybe that was also why he hadn't killed Teddy or turned him loose in the cold to freeze to death to hide his crime. Perhaps he'd even come down here to set him free, so that we'd find Teddy after Mason made his escape. He'd been willing to kill Victoria, but he hadn't wanted her dog to suffer for it.

And now I was trapped with him in a basement, and no one knew we were together.

Mason backed up two stairs. The move almost seemed casual, like he just planned to return to the main floor. But he was watching me as if he were trying to decide if I'd put the pieces together or not. I couldn't get past him if he chose not to move.

I forced out a laugh. "Finally, he's tired of barking. Took him long enough." I motioned behind me, then at Teddy. "I'll be upstairs in a minute. He must have sneaked in here when Leo came for cleaning supplies. And he left a mess that I don't want Leo to have to clean up."

Mason nodded. Something flickered across his face.

Believe me, I silently prodded him. *Go on. Go back to the others. I don't know or suspect anything.*

I put on a smile that hopefully looked more natural than a clown's. It certainly felt like a clown smile, all painted on and stiff. "Actually, could you send Leo down here? I'm not sure what he'll want me to use. I couldn't find any paper towels."

Mason glanced over at Teddy. "He was running around down here when you found him?"

Lie or tell the truth?

If I told the truth and said I found Teddy tied up, he'd know I'd lied earlier when I said Teddy had probably slipped in without Leo noticing. Which would absolutely be suspicious.

But if I lied now, he'd know I was lying. He knew he'd tied Teddy up. Tied him up well, I might add. Those knots had been tight. And Teddy clearly hadn't chewed through the leash. He was dragging an intact leash behind him as he crossed back and forth.

My stomach plunged. Mason already knew. The leash gave it away. He wasn't wearing one in his crate. So if he slipped past Leo to run down here, he shouldn't have had a leash on at all. I wouldn't have had one with me if I'd come down here for some privacy to make a phone call.

Was Mason testing me to see if I'd figured out that it was him? Or stalling because he needed time to decide how to react?

I held up my phone and shrugged. "I came down to make a call, without everyone overhearing me, and there he was."

I hadn't answered his question, but maybe he wouldn't realize it. My words kind of sounded like an answer.

"I heard your phone call."

Mason's voice was so calm. The murderers I'd encountered before hadn't been calm people. They'd been angry and passionate. They'd lunged, shot, chased.

The tone of Mason's voice when he was talking about his sister trickled back into my mind. He hadn't been calm then. He'd been bitter.

I moved my hand across the screen of my phone. Maybe I could dial Ryan, let him know I needed help.

"Please don't do that." Mason quickly stooped down and swept up a wrench that had been lying near a toolbox at the bottom of the stairs—Leo's toolbox from earlier. "Right now, it's just the two of us. You seem like you care about people. I'm hoping we can come to some sort of agreement."

What sort of agreement could we possibly come to? Stay quiet or I die? That wasn't much of an agreement. Threat, yes. Agreement, no.

But if I could keep him talking, maybe Ryan would come looking for me. He'd surely get impatient if I took too long. Especially when he couldn't find Mason.

I took a step backward, then another. "Why did you do it?"

"I don't know what you're talking about." Mason cast a pointed look at my phone, as if he wasn't convinced that I hadn't found a way to record him. "I haven't done anything. Do you mean why do I think someone would have killed Victoria? If I had to guess, that is."

I opened my mouth but nothing came out. I nodded instead. He was too smart. I wasn't going to be able to trick him into confessing—recorded, played over the phone for Ryan, or otherwise. And if Ryan did show up, it was Mason's word against mine. Based on the way he was holding that wrench, if I proved unreasonable, he was probably planning to make my death look like another accident. I'd come down here, slipped on Teddy's pee, and hit my head. What a way for someone who worked with animals to go.

"Well"—he stepped off the stairs but made sure to keep himself between me and the way out—"I gathered from what Simone was saying that Victoria likes being the other woman. She didn't seem to care about the damage that caused in the lives she left behind. The harm it caused to someone like my sister, for example. I imagine that if one of the people she'd harmed in the past found out it wasn't a one-time indiscretion, that she had an intentional pattern, they might have confronted her and demanded she stop. When she laughed in that person's face, he might have lost his temper." He smiled in a way that looked far too normal. "I wouldn't know for sure, but I could see something like that happening."

Could Victoria have been the one who broke up his sister's marriage? I bet if Ryan checked the phone records for a last name that matched Mason's sister's married name, he'd find a match. I bet if we looked at handler records for some of the dog shows prior to Victoria's affair with Mason's brother-in-law, we'd find that his brother-in-law had helped out.

Maybe Mason's rage at Victoria was partly anger at himself for introducing them in the first place.

"What she did was very wrong." I wanted to keep backing up, but if I did, he'd never believe me. I couldn't seem afraid. I wouldn't be afraid of someone I agreed with. "Victoria shouldn't have treated people that way."

He didn't move toward me. "When did it become okay to hurt other people to make yourself happy? That isn't the way I was raised."

Hurt other people.

Mason didn't seem concerned with strict right and wrong the way Graudin had been all weekend, but he was concerned about innocent people being hurt. Like a vigilante. Maybe this didn't have to end badly. Maybe that gave me a way to get through to him.

Because if I didn't, he was going to realize soon enough that he couldn't trust anything I said while he had me cornered down here. He seemed to be a thinker. He'd come up with an elaborate cover for erasing the video. It wouldn't be much longer before he figured out I was a loose end he couldn't afford.

My "accidental" death would be the safest way for him. After all, if I hadn't seen the way Teddy reacted to him, I wouldn't have put it all together. And there'd be no reason for him to hurt me if the police couldn't first prove he'd killed Victoria.

He had no criminal record. Erasing the tape "for Darcy" might only result in probation or community service. A smudge on his record compared to what a murder charge would bring.

"What about me, then?" I kept my voice soft, questioning rather than accusatory. Mason had used Simone and Darcy, but he'd also comforted and entertained them. He'd taken his sister in when she'd been in need. That hinted at a protectiveness toward women. Even his murder of Victoria could be seen as him protecting other women from her. Though, really, he should be equally furious at the men involved. They were just as guilty.

Who knew? Maybe his brother-in-law would have died in an accident a few years from now as well. Mason seemed to have that kind of patience.

Mason frowned as if he wasn't quite sure what I meant. Teddy snuffled around Mason's feet. My hands itched to grab him up in case Mason decided Teddy was also a loose end that needed to go at last.

I swallowed, moistening my dry mouth. I had to approach this carefully. No direct accusations. "And what about whoever ends up accused of Victoria's murder in place of the person who did it?"

The wrench drooped in Mason's hand, but he didn't let it drop.

"Do you think it's fair that they suffer for something someone else did? Like your sister's now suffering for something that wasn't her fault? The police are looking at Darcy. Hasn't Darcy gone through enough?"

Mason stayed perfectly still. My own breathing rattled loud in my ears.

If this didn't work, my only option would be to try to climb onto one of the tanks and call Ryan before Mason could reach me. I might be able to do it. I'd been a great tree climber as a kid. But I'd also been a lot smaller as a kid, so that was probably a pipe dream.

Mason heaved out a shuddering breath. "No. That wouldn't be fair, either." He set the wrench on the ground, sank down to sit on the step, and scratched Teddy behind the ear. He looked up at me. His eyes were bloodshot, as if he were holding back tears. "I couldn't hurt him, either. He didn't pick his owner. I wasn't going to leave him here. I just wanted him out of the way until I was gone." Teddy's back foot came off the ground and air-scratched. Mason smiled sadly. "For obvious reasons. Do you know it took me a year to earn his trust? I went over to Victoria's booth every show. I was so determined to prove I could win him over. Glen came with me. That's how they met. We had a bet about whether I could win the little guy over."

Tears were running down his cheeks now. He kept petting Teddy, as if by ignoring the tears he could pretend he wasn't crying.

I slowly lifted my phone. "May I call Detective MacIntosh? You can tell him everything so there's no chance of someone else being blamed."

Mason stuck his long legs out in front of him. "I had it all planned out. I thought if I placed a little blame here and a little blame there, the police wouldn't have enough to arrest anyone. But you're right. That's not a risk I'm willing to take." He looked up at me again. This time, his eyes were hard, the tears gone. "But I don't regret it. She really was an awful person. I don't know what Glen ever saw in her."

21

The police cruiser with Mason in the back pulled out of the convention center parking lot, another officer driving Mason's car following behind. The parking lot was the exact opposite of what it'd been yesterday evening. Where our few cars and Graudin's ridiculously oversized truck had previously huddled amid drifts of snow, the freshly plowed area was now crisscrossed with police cars, an ambulance, and vehicles for all the crime-scene personnel.

I scraped the last of the snow off my windshield. Orion followed my movements with his head from the backseat, his doggie seatbelt preventing him from climbing into the front seat, his hot breath fogging up the nearest window.

Of the original cars, only Ryan's, mine, and Darcy's still remained in the parking lot. I stayed to help dig everyone else out. Tiffany had left only ten minutes ago, Teddy in tow. Technically, he should have gone to the nearest shelter, but it wasn't no-kill or target zero. If Victoria's next of kin didn't want him, at least in Arbor he'd get the time he needed to find a new home. With enough exposure to strangers, maybe Judith could even teach him not to bark at everyone who came near him. Mason proved Teddy could learn to accept people who weren't Victoria, given enough time.

Footsteps crunched toward me on the snow, and Darcy stopped a few feet away.

Her coat was wrapped tightly around her but not buttoned. "They're letting me go since Mason's confession makes the recording unnecessary. I wanted to thank you. Your boyfriend fought for me, and I'm sure it's because he knew you wanted him to."

"He's not my..." What did it matter if Darcy thought Ryan and I were dating or not? I wouldn't see her again after this. It wasn't important enough to argue over. "You're welcome. But he would have advocated for you anyway. You were used. And not just by Mason."

She dropped her gaze to the side. "I still did things I knew were wrong. All the excuses in the world won't change that. Even though I felt like I had no other choices." She puffed out her lips. "That's another excuse. I had other choices. I just didn't like them."

Would I have made different choices? Maybe. Hopefully. But it was hard to hold on to the truth when someone kept telling you lies about yourself, over and over again, until they felt more real than the truth. When everything they did was your fault, and yet, no matter how hard you tried to fix it, it wasn't enough.

I touched her arm. "You're not responsible if he cheats. You're not making him do it. No matter what he says."

She swallowed hard enough that her throat visibly moved. "I'll still be the one to suffer for it. But I'm not going to let him push me into something I'm not comfortable with again. I found my backbone in all this mess. I'm sorry if I was witchy to everyone in the process."

She turned on her heel and picked her way over to her car. She stopped, one hand on the door handle. "You probably don't need my advice. You and the detective are good together. But I'm going to give it anyway since something useful needs to come from my mess. When you're dating someone, don't make excuses for their bad behavior. Things don't get easier after you're married."

She was in her car and gone before I could pull together a response. Setting aside the fact that she kept mistaking Ryan for my boyfriend, Keith wasn't like Darcy's husband. He wouldn't push me to do things I thought were wrong. That wasn't our problem.

My heart weighed heavy in my chest. Almost too heavy to carry. Keith and I did have one similarity with Darcy and her husband: We disagreed on so many things. Would more time change that the way Judith seemed to think? Compromise was a natural part of romantic relationships. Maybe I was being too stubborn and set in my ways.

The paramedics rolled a stretcher out the front doors,

jerking me away from my self-absorption. A dark body bag lay on top of it.

An arm linked through mine, and I jumped. My gaze snapped to the person beside me.

Simone.

"I thought I was the only one left."

Lucy poked her tiny head out of Simone's bag, blinked up at me, then vanished again. "I came back. It felt like someone should stand vigil. She might not have been the best person, but she was still a human being."

I nodded. Every person deserved to be treated with dignity because they were created in the image of God. It was why every human life had value. Why murder was wrong. The government had the authority to take a life in punishment for a crime, but no individual did. Mason, in his anger, had meted out a punishment that didn't fit Victoria's crime. Now she'd never have the chance to be anything else.

Simone and I stood side by side in silence as they loaded Victoria's body and took her away.

Simone let go of my arm, but didn't leave. She shifted her weight from one foot to the other. "Your sister is the one who runs the Arbor shelter?"

Judith had been quite visible during the event, as shelter manager, announcing events and draw winners, among other things. But most people didn't realize we were sisters. Step-sisters didn't have the advantage of genetics to help them look alike, and we didn't share the same last name.

Simone shrugged as if she'd guessed what I was thinking. "Tiffany told me after your sister called you on her phone."

"That's her. Her fiancé works there as an animal control officer as well."

Simone stuck her hand into her bag as if she needed the comfort of stroking Lucy's fur for whatever she was about to say. "I was wondering if the shelter is hiring. I still want to work with animals. I thought about trying to work as a groomer, but I see now that I don't want the stress of running my own business."

The shelter had needed more staff since the attempts on Bob's life a few months ago had scared away some of their employees. There was just one problem. "Working at the shelter is still a stressful environment a lot of the time."

Simone brought her hand back out of the bag. Lucy peeked over the edge as if not sure why she wasn't still getting petted. "I think it'll be a different kind. There must be a lot of satisfaction and joy each time an animal finds a good home."

There was that. Shelter staff still saw a lot of sick animals come in, and they saw how selfish and evil human hearts could be, but the focus was different. They also got to see animals come in bedraggled and scrawny and go out, shiny and healthy, to a loving new family. They got to play with dogs and socialize kittens. They got to hear happy adoption stories from families.

Simone gave me a tentative smile. "I'd like to try anyway. And I'm going to find a counselor rather than depending on my pills as much. In case that would be a concern."

She was looking at me so hopefully. I hadn't seen her this bright and focused since we'd "met" across Victoria's body. I pulled my phone out of my pocket. "What's your number? I'll text you Judith's contact info."

Once we were sure my text arrived, she waved goodbye, walked across the parking lot to her car, and drove away. She waved an arm out the window one last time as she pulled out. I waved back.

My phone rang. Ryan's name scrolled across my screen, still listed as *Detective MacIntosh*. I swiped my finger to answer.

"Are you free to talk?" he asked.

I climbed into my car and turned on the engine. Orion couldn't sit around in the cold any longer. "I'm still in the parking lot."

"I'll come to you."

He disconnected before I could ask any questions.

My stomach muscles clenched. Ryan wouldn't be coming to me just to say goodbye. The investigation was out of his hands now that the local authorities had taken over, but he likely still had an unreasonable number of forms to fill out and statements to give.

He knocked on the window of my car and slid into the passenger seat.

"Did you hear something about Harper?" I blurted the words out before he'd even closed the door behind him.

"I did." He tugged the door shut and held his hands out

to my car's vents even though the air coming from them wasn't much warmer yet than outside. "They haven't found her yet."

I could have guessed as much. If they'd found her, Tina would have called me. I wrapped my arms around my waist to keep from reaching for one of his hands for comfort. "Are they even looking yet?"

"They weren't." Ryan shifted in his seat so that he faced me as much as was possible in a car. "Harper has a history of running away when she's upset. She always comes back within a few days. Her foster parents think she hides out with one of her friends rather than staying on the streets."

She'd have to, with weather like we'd had. The storm wasn't localized. It'd hit all of Michigan. "Did they call her friends, looking for her?"

He nodded. "They only know one, but apparently she'll never admit when Harper's hiding out there."

"Then they can't know she's ever been there. She could be anywhere."

Ryan's hand twitched as if he were considering reaching for me, too. "Her foster father has camped out in front of the friend's house more than once until he's seen Harper there. He couldn't this time because of the storm, but they were confident she was there again. That's part of why everyone didn't seem more worried."

They shouldn't be confident. Just because Harper had done that a few times in the past didn't mean that's where she was every time. But even I had to admit that her foster parents seemed to care. Not everyone would stake out a house.

"Because she's shown a pattern of coming back, the police weren't looking for her, like I said. I asked if they'd check her friend's house as a professional courtesy. I knew you wouldn't be able to rest otherwise. I thought they'd find her, and this would all be cleared up."

I studied his face. His tone wasn't happy or relaxed like he had good news to bring me. He met my gaze. His eyes were solemn, and the corners of his mouth were tight.

"She wasn't there," I said softly.

"She wasn't there. Her friend's father let them come into the house and look for themselves. There wasn't any sign of her. Both he and his daughter said she hadn't been there. They checked the outbuildings as well."

I leaned my forehead into my steering wheel. At this point, Harper had been missing close to forty-eight hours. In the worst blizzard the state had seen in a generation. I shivered. "Are they going to issue an Amber Alert?"

Ryan's hand rested on my back, seeping his own warmth into me. "Not for a potential runaway. They only issue an Amber Alert when there's reason to think a child has been abducted."

"That's not fair."

"Maybe not, but it's practical. There's always the fear that if they issue too many Amber Alerts, people will stop paying attention."

And Harper was sixteen. Some law enforcement personnel probably assumed she was holed up somewhere with a boyfriend her foster parents didn't know about. My eyes burned. I turned my head so I could see Ryan's face. "Are they going to do anything to find her?"

"They're going to put her picture on the local news stations and online with a number to call. The idea is that someone might have seen something and call in."

Ryan's hand moved in a soothing circle. Good thing the console was between us because what I really wanted was the comfort of a hug. I wanted to crawl into his arms, put my head on his shoulder, and cry until I had nothing left inside. But I would have had to hide that from Keith because he already wasn't completely comfortable with my friendship with Ryan. Until we were broken up, I had to respect that.

I dug my nails into the steering wheel. "How long?"

Ryan's eyebrows lowered slightly, and his hand stilled. "How long what?"

I forced myself to sit up. I could face this. I had to know what I was dealing with. "How long do we have before it's likely we'll never find her? The truth."

"The first seventy-two hours are the most important for gathering evidence."

I met his eyes and waited. That wasn't what I was asking, and he knew it.

His shoulders slumped. "A week, two at most, before we stop looking for a missing person and start looking for a body."

LETTER FROM THE AUTHOR

I hope you enjoyed reading this wintery mystery as much as I enjoyed writing it.

In the next book in the Cat and Mouse Whodunits, Zoe will be trying to find Harper during one of the coldest winters Michigan has ever faced. As you might guess from the title *Catastrophe*, cats will be involved!

If you haven't yet signed up for my newsletter, please do. I announce new releases there first, as well as sharing recipes and other fun bonuses. I also give my newsletter subscribers a free ebook copy of *Sapped*, a Maple Syrup Mysteries prequel.

You can sign up at www.smarturl.it/emilyjames.

Love,

Emily

ABOUT THE AUTHOR

Emily James grew up watching TV shows like *Matlock*, *Monk*, and *Murder She Wrote*. (It's pure coincidence that they all begin with an M.) It was no surprise to anyone when she turned into a mystery writer.

Alongside being a writer, she's also a baker, an animal lover, and a musician.

Emily and her husband share their home with a Boxer mix, nine cats (all rescues), and a budgie (who is both the littlest and the loudest).

If you'd like to know as soon as Emily's next mystery releases, please join her newsletter list at www.smarturl.it/emilyjames.